Ruby Lee & Me

Shannon Hitchcock

Scholastic Press / New York

Photos (pp. 214–217) courtesy of the author, except: aerial view of grandparents' farm (p. 214) courtesy of Tracy Williams; Mrs. Porter (p. 216) courtesy of Mrs. Pauline Porter's family

Laced linen frames of horse embroidery (pp. 216–217): de-kay/istockphoto

Copyright © 2016 by Shannon Hitchcock

All rights reserved. Published by Scholastic Press, an imprint of Scholastic Inc., *Publishers since 1920.* SCHOLASTIC, SCHOLASTIC PRESS, and associated logos are trademarks and/or registered trademarks of Scholastic Inc.

The publisher does not have any control over and does not assume any responsibility for author or third-party websites or their content.

No part of this publication may be reproduced, stored in a retrieval system, or transmitted in any form or by any means, electronic, mechanical, photocopying, recording, or otherwise, without written permission of the publisher. For information regarding permission, write to Scholastic Inc., Attention: Permissions Department, 557 Broadway, New York, NY 10012.

This book is a work of fiction. Names, characters, places, and incidents are either the product of the author's imagination or are used fictitiously, and any resemblance to actual persons, living or dead, business establishments, events, or locales is entirely coincidental.

Library of Congress Cataloging-in-Publication Data available

ISBN 978-0-545-78230-2

10 9 8 7 6 5 4 3 2 1 16 17 18 19 20

Printed in the U.S.A. 23

First edition, January 2016

Book design by Carol Ly

In memory of Mrs. Pauline Porter, who first taught me to read, and my sister, Robin, who once said, "Make up a story about us."

CHAPTER ONE

The Accident

It was a perfectly ordinary day, until it wasn't.

Robin played in the sandbox while I read underneath the mimosa tree. I was spending the first day of summer vacation babysitting my sister, or at least I was supposed to be. Before long my mind had drifted clear out of North Carolina, and I was swimming with a dolphin off the English coast.

A loud screech jolted me out of the story. A car, a black car, had hit someone! Bad things *never* happened in our neighborhood. I hid my face in my hands. It couldn't be real.

When I got the courage to look, people were spilling from cars and homes into the street. I dropped my book and ran toward them.

A man I didn't know took charge. "Call an ambulance," he shouted. "Somebody call an ambulance!"

I saw Robin's red tennis shoe abandoned in the street. I yelled. I cried and wailed. She lay on the ground, small and still. When I screamed her name, she tried to get up. Her legs crumpled beneath her.

I got all cold and numb, like I'd been put in the meat locker at Gentry's Grocery. A faraway ambulance siren rang in my ears.

Mama gave me a hard shake. "Sarah, listen to me."

I tried to focus on her face, but it was a blur. Instead I stared at Mama's hands. They were still dirty from working in the vegetable garden.

"I have to go with Robin in the ambulance," Mama said. "Stay with Cathy until I get back."

I was terrified for the ambulance to take Robin away. I might never see her again.

I pulled from Mama's grasp and hurried to where the paramedics were loading Robin onto a stretcher. With her eyes closed, she didn't look six years old. She looked like a baby.

I fell to my knees. Why did this have to happen? Why?

Chapter Two

Grandpa's House

The ambulance sped away, and our neighbor Cathy helped me to my feet. "You're trembling," she said. "I'm gonna wrap you in a warm quilt and make you a cup of tea."

A quilt and tea? That wouldn't fix things. Nothing could.

I took a last look at the scene of the accident. A policeman was questioning the driver whose car had hit Robin. He looked about eighteen, Cathy's age, and kept tugging at his shirt collar. A red-hot hatred ran through me. I wished I could kick him, scratch him, bite him. I would never forgive him for hurting my sister, not in a million, billion years.

Cathy put her arm around me and led me from the street to her house. Though she piled quilts on me, I was freezing from the inside out. My teeth chattered. Her dog, Scruffy, burrowed under the covers and cuddled up with me.

The phone rang, and Cathy ran to answer it. "Yes, yes, sir," she said. "Don't worry. I know I sound young, but I used to babysit Sarah. Yeah, I think she's doing okay. She's wrapped in a quilt and sipping some tea."

Cathy stayed on the phone a long time and then hung up the receiver. "That was your grandpa. He's coming to get you."

"Why?"

She picked at her fingernails and didn't look at me directly. "Because your parents are spending the night at the hospital. Your grandparents want you to stay with them until Robin's better."

I hid my face in Scruffy's fur. Ever since Grandpa called, Cathy's eyes were swimming in tears. I was scared to ask why.

At five thirty, Cathy's mama got home from working in the hosiery mill. She fussed over me and made a meat loaf, but my stomach churned. I pretended to be asleep, so I wouldn't have to eat it.

Just after supper, Grandpa shuffled in, wearing his Old Hickory overalls. I flung the quilts aside and barreled into him, nearly knocking him off his feet. He patted my hair. "How's my girl?"

"I'm afraid, Grandpa."

"Me too," he whispered. He thanked Cathy and her mama for taking care of me. "We surely appreciate it." He promised to call whenever he had more news. Then Grandpa turned to me. "We need to get you packed up," he said.

Our house was quiet, except for a running toilet. I wiggled the handle until it stopped, and then hurried down the hall to my bedroom. I called it *the lavender library*, because the walls were purple, and it was full of books. I packed my clothes, then stuffed sandals and a pair of Keds underneath them. There was only room left for my journal and a few novels. I stood in front of my bookshelf, thinking about which ones I might need. Finally I chose *Little House on the Prairie*, *Heidi Grows Up*, and *The Wizard of Oz*.

I lugged the heavy suitcase to Robin's room. It was decorated with Western stuff, because she wanted to be a cowgirl when she grew up. I took a picture of Robin wearing a cowboy hat off her dresser. I wrapped it in a towel and placed it in my suitcase.

Grandpa's dog, Rowdy, was waiting in the back of the truck. He barked and wagged his tail. I was glad to see him.

"You don't mind if I put your suitcase in the back with Rowdy, do you?"

"Course not. He can't hurt that old suitcase."

"I'll get your bike," Grandpa said. "You might be staying with us for a while."

A while sounded like a long time. I wanted the doctors to make Robin better and send her home tomorrow or, better yet, right now.

Night settled in, and the sky would be black as pitch before we reached the farm. Grandpa rolled his window down, and a warm breeze blew in. We left the small town of Tucker behind and traveled down a country road with no streetlights. Grandpa sang "In the Sweet By-and-By." He had a wonderful, deep voice. Listening to him soothed me like a lullaby. I could almost pretend the accident hadn't happened.

When he finished the song, Grandpa said, "Sweet pea, what happened today?"

I didn't know how to answer him. I saw the accident, but my memories were jumbled. At first I didn't know

Robin was hurt. I just thought she had wandered off. And then when I saw her lying on the ground, it felt the way Reverend Reece describes hell when he's all wound up.

"Sarah?"

Grandpa was waiting for me to explain, but I didn't know how to own up to a mistake that big. Finally, I took the easy way out. "Robin ran and I couldn't catch her in time."

"Where was she going?" Grandpa asked.

"I don't know. Could we not talk about it? Please."

Grandpa reached into his pocket and handed me a handkerchief. "Maybe you'll feel more like talking tomorrow."

I didn't think so.

It grew even darker on Shady Creek Road. The pavement ended, and Grandpa's red truck bumped along on the gravel. There were no signs and no streetlights. We passed the shadows of cow pastures, tobacco barns, and cornfields.

"Dang it," Grandpa said. "Now I can't see at all. Can you drive from here?" Grandpa needed an operation for cataracts, but so far he'd been too stubborn to get one.

Grandpa pulled over, and I changed seats with him. Though I was only twelve, that didn't matter on a farm. I had been driving ever since my feet could reach the pedals. A few minutes later, I turned into the farmhouse driveway and shifted into park.

"Mighty fine driving job," Grandpa said. "It's good to be home."

It surely was. Though I didn't live there, the farm felt like a second home to me. Granny had left the front-porch light on for us, but only the moon shone on the barn and outbuildings. I usually visited the farm with Robin. I had a baseball-size lump in my throat.

Granny was waiting in the kitchen. She smelled like fresh-baked biscuits, and when she hugged me, her faded housedress felt soft against my cheek. "I bet you haven't had anything to eat," she said. My granny thought a hot meal would help almost any problem.

I told Granny I wasn't hungry, but she didn't let that stop her. "A little bit of chicken soup will make you feel better. It'll warm you up and calm your stomach." Granny ladled soup into a bowl and crumbled saltine crackers on top. "Now eat it real slow."

It was easier to do it Granny's way than to argue. When I finished, she led me to the bathroom and drew a tubful of warm water. "Climb in and take a nice, long soak," she said. "I'll be back directly to check on you."

My arms and legs relaxed in the warm water. I closed my eyes and wished it could wash away the accident, suck it right down the drain like it had never happened.

Sometime much later, Granny knocked on the door. "Can I come in?"

My skin had shriveled like a dried apple. "Yeah, I need to dry off." Granny handed me a fluffy towel, and I burrowed into its softness. I perched on the commode while Granny worked a comb through my tangled hair.

"You forgot to pack a nightgown, so you'll have to sleep in one of mine."

It had been a long time since I had let anybody take care of me like that. I followed Granny to the big bed, climbed in, and pulled the quilt up to my chin. "Dear Lord," Granny prayed. "Thank you for both of my granddaughters. Please watch over them tonight. I don't understand why this terrible thing has happened, but I'm trusting you to get us through it. Amen." She bent down and gave me a goodnight kiss.

All alone, I couldn't sleep in the big bed. I thought about Granny's prayer. Her faith was strong, but I had trouble believing in things I couldn't see.

My arms felt empty, and I wanted to hug Robin so much it hurt. I climbed out of bed and took her picture from my suitcase. Clutching the frame to my chest, I knelt by the window.

The farmyard was covered by moonlight. When I was little, I used to wish upon a star. I closed my eyes and wished for two things. The first was for Robin to be good as new. And though my second wish was impossible, I wished it with all my heart. Somehow, I wished the accident hadn't been my fault.

Chapter Three

Bread Baking

I woke to the rooster crowing. For a few seconds, I didn't even know why I was on the farm, but then I remembered. Robin was hurt. She could even be dead.

I hid underneath the covers while the accident played inside my mind like a horror movie. Robin's body slammed against the pavement; the siren wailed. I curled up like a ball of yarn. Maybe if I rolled up tight enough, I'd feel safe.

Granny pulled the covers back and gathered me into her arms. "Sssh," she whispered. "Don't cry. It'll be all right. Everything will be all right."

When I finally quieted down, Granny said, "Robin's still unconscious. They'll know more about her head injury when she wakes up."

Robin was alive! Those words were as sweet as an angel's singing.

"I want you to get dressed," Granny said. "I'm gonna teach you to make my prizewinning biscuits. Ain't nothing in this world more soothing than making biscuits."

Granny walked over to the cupboard by the sink and took down a wooden recipe box. "Grandpa made this for you a while back," she said. "I've been waiting for the right time to give it to you."

The box was made of maple wood and had *Sarah's Recipes* carved on the lid. "Grandpa did a beautiful job. I'll always keep it."

"I'm glad you like it," Granny said. "I thought you would."

Following her directions, I sifted two cups of self-rising flour. I threw in a dollop of lard about the size of a hen's egg. I worked in the lard, then slowly added buttermilk.

Granny peered over my shoulder. "Buttermilk's the secret to good biscuits," she said.

Getting the dough just right was harder than it looked. First my dough was too gooey, and then it was too dry.

"Don't get frustrated," Granny said. "Find your rhythm. Focus on your hands and the dough."

Making biscuits relaxed me like a warm bath.

Once the bread was in the oven, I had a question for Granny that had been gnawing at my insides. "How do I get through something this awful?"

Granny turned from crumbling sausage in the skillet for gravy. She stared at me a while before answering. "Every sorrow is different, but you get through 'em the same way. Plenty of rest, good food, and keeping your family and friends close by." She paused for a minute. "A lot of prayer doesn't hurt either."

I thought about all Granny had said. I knew she prayed for us every single day, but that didn't stop bad things from happening. Nothing could.

The screen door banged shut, and Grandpa carried in a full pail of milk. With every footstep, he tracked mud and manure across the kitchen floor. Granny grabbed her broom. "Look at those muddy brogans," she scolded. "Out, out of my kitchen."

I cracked a smile. Grandpa almost never remembered to wipe his feet.

At the sound of crunching gravel, Granny hurried over to the window. "It's your daddy," she said.

I knocked over my orange juice.

Dad's eyes settled on each of us gathered around the table: first Grandpa, then Granny, and finally, on me. "The doctors didn't expect Robin to make it through the night," he said, "but she proved them wrong. Robin's always been a fighter."

I gripped the oak table so hard my knuckles turned white.

Steam rose from the stove, and Granny bustled over to turn off the burners. "Have mercy," she said. "I almost ruined breakfast." Though nobody had much of an appetite, she broke open a biscuit and spooned sausage gravy over the top. She placed the plate down in front of my dad. "Charlie, not another word until you get some food in your stomach." She filled more plates and told Grandpa and me to eat too so we'd keep our strength up.

Dad took a couple of bites, but mostly he just sipped coffee. I kept my grip on the table, and my eyes never left his face. "There's no easy way to say this," he said. "It's a bad sign that Robin's still unconscious. And the longer she is, the more serious it looks."

Granny pulled a handkerchief from her apron pocket and wiped her eyes. "What else?" she asked.

"She has a collapsed lung," Dad said. He sounded like he was reading from a medical encyclopedia. Dad was a lot more comfortable talking about car engines than dealing with doctors.

"What are they doing about it?" Grandpa asked.

Dad raked his hands through his light-brown hair. "The doctor put a chest tube in." Then Dad patted his thigh. "And her femur is broken. That's the big bone right here."

I thought about how much Robin liked to run and jump and climb. "But the leg's not a big deal, right? Can't they just put a cast on it?"

Dad looked down at the table. "It'll take a year or more for her leg to heal. But right now, the leg doesn't matter much. What matters is that she opens those beautiful brown eyes of hers."

I knew that a year would seem like forever to Robin. "Dad, when do the doctors think she'll wake up?"

He kept looking down at the table and didn't meet my eyes. "There's no way of knowing," he said. "No way at all."

CHAPTER FOUR

Berry Picking

After Dad left for the hospital, I curled up on the den couch with an afghan. Cleaning sounds kept me company: running water, a swishing broom, and banging cupboards. I didn't have the energy to help Granny with her chores. I wished that I could fall asleep and not wake up until Robin was back home again.

For lunch, Granny made chicken pie, one of my favorites. I ate exactly one forkful and pushed my plate away.

"Honey, you should try to eat," Grandpa said.

I moved some peas around with my fork and didn't answer.

Once the plates were washed and dripping in the dish drainer, Granny said, "Sarah Beth, grab a bucket. We're gonna pick blackberries with Miss Irene and Ruby Lee."

I shook my head no, but Granny had already made up her mind. She said waiting for the phone to ring was driving us both crazy as bedbugs. Granny reached for her bonnet on a hook by the back door. "The fresh air will do you good."

We set off for the berry patch, with Granny swinging her hoe and me trailing behind. Granny belonged in the Little House on the Prairie books with her bonnet and hoe.

Chickens squawked as we passed by the henhouse. Before long the chicken smell was replaced by the scent of flue-cured tobacco. It reminded me of a pipe only stronger. Though it would be another month before it was time to cure tobacco, the smell had seeped into the old wooden barns. I remembered the last time I was here. Robin and Rowdy had been with me.

Miss Irene and her granddaughter, Ruby Lee, were already picking berries when we got to the patch. Granny and Miss Irene had an arrangement. Miss Irene helped Granny butcher hogs, make quilts, and can vegetables. In return, Grandpa delivered milk and eggs to Miss Irene, and shared her vegetable garden and fruit trees.

"Lawd, child, you have been through a hard time," Miss Irene said. She wrapped me in her strong brown arms. I had always loved Miss Irene, and Ruby too, but there was a fine line between our families. Granny and Miss Irene gossiped like best friends here on the farm, but only nodded and smiled when they saw each other in town. I had asked Granny about it once and she said, "The creek don't care what color feet wade in it, but the town pool surely does. It's easier to be friends away from wagging tongues."

Ruby and me took our pails to the far end of the patch, away from our grandmothers. Ruby moved like a ballet dancer, slim and graceful. "How you doing?" she asked.

My eyes started to flood, and I wiped away tears. "Not too good."

"Umm hmm," Ruby said. "I can see that. Want to talk about it?"

I answered no, but if I ever did talk about the accident, it would be to Ruby.

She stuffed some berries into her mouth and held out her palms for me to see. They were stained a deep purple. "These berries taste like heaven," she said, "heaven and sunshine."

I dropped some berries into my bucket, and then ate a handful too. Ruby sang a spiritual while we filled our pails nearly full. She was a soloist at the Open Arms Baptist Church and made up lots of songs.

Pick me up, Lord

Trouble's too hard to bear

Pick me up, Lord

Show me you care.

I wished I could spend all day in the berry patch listening to Ruby, but Granny and Miss Irene's squabbling interrupted.

"I'll do it. I'll do it for you," Miss Irene said. She picked up her own pail of berries and Granny's too.

"You don't need to carry both buckets," Granny said.

Miss Irene insisted. "No trouble. No trouble at all."

Ruby scowled. It embarrassed her when Miss Irene tried too hard around white people. If you ask me, that's why Ruby was a tad bossy. She didn't want to be like Miss Irene.

Back in the kitchen, Granny sat down and propped her right leg on a footstool. The veins bulged out like a knotted rope underneath her skin. "My leg is bothering me again," she said. "I'm gonna sit right here and let you make the cobbler."

Following Granny's directions, I scooped two cups of

berries into the bowl. “Pour right much sugar over them,” Granny said. “That makes them nice and sweet.”

“How much is right much?”

“Oh, ’bout half a cup.”

Granny rubbed her leg. “I got these varicose veins when I was pregnant with your daddy.”

Granny’s skin looked thin and shiny, like her veins could bust right through the skin. “That was a long time ago. Why didn’t they get well?”

“I don’t know,” Granny said. “Just never did. I guess I could show ’em to the doctor, but I’m like your grandpa with his cataracts. I don’t like doctors working on me.”

I looked up from stirring the melted butter. “What about the doctors working on Robin?”

“That’s a whole different story,” Granny said. “Robin’s injuries are life-threatening.”

Life-threatening. Those words sucked the air out of the kitchen. Neither Granny nor me moved a muscle. Finally, I whispered, “I’m afraid she’ll die.”

Granny took off her glasses and wiped her eyes with a handkerchief. "Sarah, turn off the stove. We need to talk."

I knelt on the floor beside Granny's stool, and she stroked my hair. "We're all scared. Scared plumb to death, but we've gotta take it one day at a time. Keeping busy will help us through the rough patches." Granny paused. "Do you want to talk about the day of the accident?"

I shook my head.

"I won't try and make you," Granny said, "but I think you'd feel better if you'd talk about it. Remember when you got that splinter in your backside sliding down the banister?"

"Yes, ma'am. Almost two years ago, when I was ten."

Granny nodded. "You wouldn't let me get the splinter out and it festered. That sore got worse and worse, until I dug the splinter out with a needle. The bad feelings inside of you are a lot like that splinter."

I knew my granny was like King Solomon in the Bible, full of wisdom, but I couldn't tell her what happened. I wanted to, but the truth stuck to my throat like lumpy mashed potatoes.

The phone rang while I was washing dishes. *News . . . what if it's bad news?* A soapy mixing bowl slipped from my hands. It shattered against the porcelain sink and slivers of glass flew. I ran straight through them. "Hello," I panted.

Dad's voice answered me. "Hey, Sarah, are you hanging in there? Listening to your grandparents?"

My heartbeat slowed to its normal thud. Dad wouldn't be making small talk if Robin had gotten worse. "How is she?"

Dad sighed, and his breath came out in a loud whoosh. "About the same. She's still unconscious. I just called to check on you."

I twisted the phone cord around my finger. "I want to see her." Dad didn't answer, and for just a minute I wondered if we had been disconnected. "Dad? Are you there?"

"I don't think that's a good idea," he finally said. "Let's wait until she wakes up."

"But, Dad . . ."

"Sarah, I need to go. The doctor just walked in to examine Robin. Tell your grandparents there's been no change. I love you." And before I had the chance to say another word, he hung up.

Granny stood in the doorway between the kitchen and den, listening. "Robin's all bruised and banged up. Your daddy's afraid the way she looks will upset you."

"Not seeing her upsets me more."

"I know it does. Be patient, and I'll have a talk with your daddy about it." Granny motioned toward the bathroom. "Child, we need to get your feet bandaged up. You ran right through broken glass."

I didn't even feel it.

Chapter Five

Good Books

I woke up long before the rooster crowed. I had dreamed about Robin again, but in this dream I had been reading Robin's favorite book to her, about Billy and his horse, Blaze. I knew the dream was a sign, and that I was supposed to read the book to her.

I tiptoed across the linoleum floor, careful not to wake up my grandparents. I was already kneading the biscuit dough when Granny hobbled into the kitchen. "You're up early," she said.

"I couldn't sleep, so I'm making biscuits."

"It's a treat when somebody else does the cooking," Granny said. She tied on her apron, walked over, and peered into the refrigerator. "What about some bacon and eggs to go with those biscuits?"

I still didn't have much appetite, but I said yes. I wanted to be so agreeable that Granny and Grandpa would take me to the library, and then to the hospital. I waited until Grandpa was on his second cup of coffee to ask. "Would you give me a ride to the library this morning? I need to check out some books."

Grandpa reached for another biscuit. "I guess I could do that. Drop you off, and then do some banking. Maybe even swap a few lies down at the general store."

I took a deep breath. "Do you believe in signs?"

"What kind of signs?" Granny asked.

I told them about my dream. About how I needed to see Robin and read the Billy and Blaze books to her.

Granny nodded. "Lots of people had dreams in the Bible." She glanced up at the clock above the stove. "The library doesn't open until ten. That gives us time to wash the dishes and do up the chores." She carried the plates over to the sink. "Well, George, get a move on. Sarah's on a mission."

We left the farm behind with Grandpa driving, Granny riding next to the window, and me squished in the middle. Rowdy was in the back, like always. Grandpa's truck would only go about thirty-five miles per hour, so it would be a slow trip.

"In town, all the roads have street signs," I said. "No wonder people get lost out here."

Grandpa adjusted the rearview mirror. "I've been meaning to have a sign painted and put it out by the main road. That way folks from town won't miss the turnoff. Guess the farm would need a name though."

"Just call it *Willis Family Farm*," Granny said. "No need to get uppity about it."

Though I'd only had a couple of bites of breakfast, my stomach churned. I pressed both hands against it.

Granny eyed my middle. "Do you have an upset stomach?"

"Just a little bit."

Granny pulled off her glasses and wiped the lenses with her housedress. "Sarah, you need to be prepared for what you're gonna see. Robin is all bandaged up, she has an IV in her hand, a tube for oxygen in her nose, and her leg is hanging in traction. Your parents didn't want you to see her like this, but I told them you're a big girl. That you'll be able to handle it."

I squeezed my eyes shut. I didn't want to see *this* Robin. I wanted to see the sister I had before the accident, but one thing I knew for sure: I had to read to Robin, hold her hand, and beg her to please, please wake up.

Grandpa started singing "Will the Circle Be Unbroken." Dad, Mama, Robin, and me made a perfect family circle. I worried we'd be broken apart.

We pulled into the library just as it was opening. I fished my library card out of my pocket. It was quiet inside and smelled musty, like paper, ink, and old books. I was the first customer.

Mrs. Brown whispered from behind the front desk, "Good morning, Sarah."

"Good morning," I whispered back. I loved Mrs. Brown because she enjoyed answering my questions, but this morning I didn't have time to talk. I knew exactly which books I needed.

I squatted down among the picture books and grabbed all of the Billy and Blaze series by C. W. Anderson. These books were Robin's favorites, and I had read them to her so many times, I almost knew them by heart.

Next I went to the 811 section for poetry. I pulled *Sonnets from the Portuguese*, by Elizabeth Barrett Browning. Cathy had read one of the poems to me when she was taking senior English. "How do I love thee? Let me count the ways." I had always loved my sister, but before the accident, I didn't know how much.

Outside Robin's hospital door, I traced one of the book covers with my finger. My heart was beating so loud that I was surprised no one else could hear it.

Granny gave my hand a gentle squeeze. "Grandpa and me will be waiting for you right here, right outside this door, but take your time. Say what you need to say to your sister."

When I pushed open the door, Mama stood up and met me in the middle of the room. I noticed lots of things at once. Mama needed to comb her hair, she didn't have on any makeup, and her clothes were rumpled. Mama opened her arms and gave me a big hug. Both of us were trembling.

Mama stepped away, and I saw Robin for the first time since the accident. Just as Granny had warned me . . . she, my sister, my baby sister had a tube in her nose, an IV in her hand, her chest and head were bandaged, and her poor leg was hanging in a sling. I clutched the library books to my chest and sobbed.

"Sssh," Mama said. "We don't know how much Robin can hear or understand while she's unconscious. If you cry, it might scare her."

I wiped my face with a Kleenex from Robin's bedside table. I stared at her a long time before I pulled a chair close to the bed and started to read. "Billy was a little boy who loved horses more than anything else in the world." My voice shook at first, but the longer I read, the stronger it got. Robin didn't move or open her eyes, but I knew she could hear me. Don't ask me how I knew. I just did.

When I finished the last book, I put a kiss as soft as rose petals on Robin's cheek. I thought of all the many ways I loved her. Like Elizabeth Barrett Browning, I should write them down. I loved reading to Robin, loved her brown curly hair, how cute she looked in her cowboy hat, how kind she was to animals, even the way she stomped her foot when she was having a temper tantrum. "I love you to the end of the universe and back," I said.

"Please wake up soon. Everybody is miserable." I slid my index finger underneath Robin's hand, and for just a second, her fingers moved.

"Did you see that? Her fingers moved!"

Mama sighed. "That's probably wishful thinking on your part. She's been unresponsive since we got here."

I stubbornly shook my head. "She touched me. I know she did."

Mama pulled a tissue from her pocket and wiped her face. "I'd give anything if you're right, but I'm afraid to get my hopes up."

"It wasn't just wishful thinking. It really happened."

A smile flickered across Mama's face. "Maybe it's a good thing you're here. Dad and I were trying to protect you, but I think Robin needs you right now."

"I need her too." I handed the Billy and Blaze books to Mama. "Keep reading these to her. Read them over and over."

Mama promised.

Chapter Six

The Power of Prayer

Seeing Robin left me as wrung out as an old dish-rag. For the first time since the accident, I slept without dreaming. When I finally got up, I had a late Sunday breakfast—warm biscuits and blackberry jam.

Granny had pressed my favorite lavender skirt for church and hung it on the door between the kitchen and den. I got dressed and caught my long, blond hair into a ponytail. I stared at myself in the mirror, wishing I didn't have quite so many freckles.

When I was ready, I knocked on Granny's bedroom door. "Can I come in?"

Granny didn't answer. Instead there was a strange noise. "*Uuummm, uuummm. Uuummm, uuugggh.*"

I pushed the door open, worried Granny was having a stroke or a heart attack. There she was—tugging on her girdle for all she was worth.

I looked down at the floor to keep from giggling. Robin should be here to see it too. She thought underwear and potty jokes were the funniest things in the world.

After Granny got the torturous girdle around her middle, she flopped down in a chair. "I'm plumb worn-out, and I still have to get my stockings on."

I sat on the edge of the bed while Granny put a stocking on each leg and fastened them to her garters. Then Granny slipped into a navy polyester dress. "How about zipping me up?" she asked. To finish off her ensemble, Granny pinned a pearl brooch on her right shoulder. "I'm ready." She beamed.

We dodged the chicken poop in the yard and climbed into Grandpa's old red truck. Rowdy had his usual spot in the back.

As we chugged down the dirt road, Grandpa said, "I think Rowdy likes church music. When they keep the windows open, he can hear the whole service."

Granny laughed. "Don't kid yourself. That dog just likes to ride. He ain't one bit picky about the destination."

Almost everybody went to church in Shady Creek. The parking lot was nearly full. To keep Rowdy comfortable, Grandpa parked in a shady spot underneath a row of maple trees. Granny waved at Hiram Fletcher, their closest neighbor, and I waved at my friend Betsy Carter.

I shuffled behind Granny and Grandpa to the front door. Most of these folks looked out of place to me. I was used to seeing the farmers in overalls instead of stiff white shirts and shiny shoes. Some of the women even wore hats. Mrs. Fletcher's looked like a bird's nest.

My favorite thing about church was the stained-glass windows. They reminded me of Joseph's coat of many colors. The organist played softly, and everyone spoke in hushed tones.

Mrs. Carter hugged Granny. "How's your grandbaby doing?" she asked.

"She's still unconscious," Granny said. "Keep praying."

Mrs. Fletcher bent down and hugged me. "You poor thing," she said. "You poor, poor thing. We're all praying for you."

I didn't like for anybody to hug me except for family, but today I didn't mind.

Granny and Grandpa led the way to our seats. Betsy Carter left her family and moved to sit beside me. I had met her last year at Vacation Bible School. At first I couldn't believe somebody so beautiful wanted to be my friend, but we had been the only two girls in a roomful of boys.

I didn't pay much attention during announcements, but then my ears perked up. "Today is a special Sunday," the preacher said. "For the past few weeks we've been focused on our boys serving in Vietnam, but today we've got trouble a little closer to home. Most of you already know that Robin Willis was injured in an automobile accident. For anybody that's wondering, she's George and Maybelle's granddaughter."

And my sister, I silently added.

Reverend Reece continued, "We don't understand why bad things happen, but the good Lord promises to never leave us or forsake us."

"Amen," Granny said.

Reverend Reece bobbed his head in her direction. "Our service will be a little different today. I'm going to ask Blanche to come on up and play 'Just as I Am' on the organ. I'd like for everybody to gather and pray at the altar."

I followed Granny and Grandpa to the front of the church. We knelt at the altar, and the whole congregation crowded around us.

Mr. Fletcher was the first one to pray. "Please take care of her, Lord."

A man with a crew cut said, "I went to school with Charlie Willis. He's a fine fellow, and I hate to see his family suffering."

I felt a jolt of electricity running along our clasped hands. As I knelt between Granny and Grandpa, I could almost believe in miracles. I wished that I could actually hear God's voice, or see a sign, like Moses and the burning bush. That would make faith a lot easier to come by.

At the end of the hour, Reverend Reece closed with a prayer. "Lord, your will be done. You know what we're asking. But we realize there are three possible answers to a prayer: yes, no, or wait."

There was only one answer that I wanted. I was sick of waiting, and I couldn't stand it if the answer was no. I wanted to yell at Reverend Reece to only pray for yes, but a hickory switch would be waiting on me if I caused a scene. My dad believed in "spare the rod and spoil the child."

Betsy opened the door to Grandpa's truck. "I thought you'd be out here. I promised your granny that I'd get you something to eat. There's a potluck dinner in the fellowship hall."

"Oh. I was hoping we were going home."

"That would be kinda rude," Betsy said. "The potluck dinner is for your family."

I didn't care about being rude. I wanted to kick Reverend Reece in the shin and make him take his prayer back.

"It's hot in this truck," Betsy said. "Let's sit on the back steps to eat. There's fried chicken, ham biscuits, potato salad, the works."

My stomach growled because I hadn't eaten very much since the accident. "What's for dessert?"

Betsy grinned and counted them off on her fingers. "Coconut pie, pecan pie, egg custard, strawberry shortcake, pound cake, German chocolate cake, and Jell-O salad."

I followed Betsy to the steps, but no way was I going any farther. I didn't want to be called a "poor, poor thing," and hear everybody whispering about my family.

"No problem," Betsy said. "I'll get the food."

I ate a chicken leg, a couple of bites of macaroni, and then pushed the plate away.

"You didn't eat very much," Betsy said.

I sipped sweet tea, hoping the sick feeling in my stomach would pass. "I can't eat, and I'm not sleeping so good either." I looked off toward the cemetery. Six generations of the Willis family were buried out there.

Betsy looked off toward the cemetery too. "Sarah, there's something I need to tell you." The cup shook in her hand. "Jason Shore, the boy who was driving, he's my sister's boyfriend. He was in the service this morning."

My hands clenched into fists. "He hurt my sister. Why would he come here?"

"Reverend Reece invited him. Jason feels guilty. He

can't eat or sleep either. Reverend Reece thought it might help if he apologized to your family."

I shook my head. "It's not like he broke my doll, or cheated off my test paper." My voice got louder. "Do you know what I saw yesterday? My sister can't talk or even open her eyes! I wish he were the one in the hospital and Robin was here with me." I scrambled to my feet.

"Where are you going?" Betsy asked.

"Out to the tombstones."

"Want me to go with you?"

I shook my head. "No, not this time."

I hurried out to my family's plot. I had been there many times before with Granny to put flowers on the graves. There were tombstones of all sizes. The small ones were usually for children. Granny had told me that before vaccinations were common, lots of kids died from diseases like diphtheria. I leaned back against my great-uncle John's monument, remembering the day of his funeral. He had been so old, eighty-five, arthritic and gray. Granny said death had eased his suffering. I thought the funeral of a child would be different than Uncle John's, even sadder. And if it were Robin, I would miss her for the rest of my life. I needed to talk to Ruby Lee about it. Ruby knew about dying, and unlike most grown-ups, she wouldn't sugarcoat the truth.

Chapter Seven

Down the Ravine

If you ask me, Sunday afternoons are the most boring time of the week. Granny dozed in the recliner, and Grandpa napped underneath the maple trees. I stretched across my bed and tried reading *Heidi Grows Up*, but after five pages, the words blurred together.

I threw the book down on the bed and opened my journal. I read through a bedtime story that I had been writing for Robin. I had never finished it, and now it might be too late.

On a blank page, I wrote the words that I was too ashamed to say out loud. *Robin's accident is my fault.* I yanked the page out and tore it into a thousand pieces. Better to use pig Latin. *Obin'sray accidentway asway ymay aultfay.* I wrote it over and over, like the time our teacher made the class write sentences for being too noisy. I didn't stop until my fingers cramped.

I left a note for Granny on the kitchen table. *Gone to Ruby's house. Be back soon. Love, Sarah.*

I climbed on my bike and followed the path deep in the woods until I came to a small white house. Instead of planting grass, Miss Irene had turned her front yard into a flower garden. Ruby was rocking on the front-porch swing.

"You thirsty?" she asked.

I put the kickstand down on my bike. "Yep. It's hot as blazes."

We rocked on the porch swing, sipping sweet tea. "Where's Miss Irene?" I asked.

"Napping," Ruby answered. "Ain't that what most grown-ups do on Sunday afternoons? Seems like a waste of a perfectly good day to me."

"That's what I think too. Where's your uncle Clarence?"

"He's gone fishing." Ruby grinned. "I wouldn't wanna be Clarence when he gets back here. He skipped church. You know how Ma Rene feels about that."

Miss Irene might have kowtowed to white people, but she was the boss in her own family.

"What have you been doing since church?" Ruby asked.

"I tried to read, but I couldn't make sense of the words."

Ruby nodded like she got what I was talking about. "I was that way after my daddy was killed in Vietnam. Had to repeat fourth grade because of it."

"I remember that. It's why I'm here. I'm afraid Robin will, you know . . ."

"Die," said Ruby Lee.

I took a deep breath and let it out. "That's what I'm most afraid of."

Ruby chewed on her lip. "If she dies, you'll be sad for a long time, but then one day you'll eat some chocolate cake and it'll taste good again, or you'll laugh at *The Beverly Hillbillies*. Somehow you'll start feeling better, even if you don't want to."

"But there's no way to be as happy as before. Is there?"

Ruby shook her head. "Nope, don't see how. I still miss my daddy every day. Some stuff can't be fixed."

I didn't feel like going back to the farm. I turned my bike in the direction of Moccasin Gap, pedaling hard up the steep hill. Sweat dripped down my back and under my arms. I rode by a deep gulley that folks had used as a junkyard. It was filled with hubcaps, a wringer washing machine, even an old car. Shady Creek had a perfectly good junkyard. I thought more people should use it. Granny said littering folks hadn't been raised right.

About a mile from home, a truck pulled up behind me. Its engine breathed down my neck. Gravel crackled. It reminded me of Robin's accident. I stayed close to the edge of the road and kept pedaling. Then the horn blared.

I looked over my shoulder, and my bike veered off the road. Screaming like a wild animal, I headed down the ravine. The bike picked up speed, and I flew over the handlebars.

"Sarah, Sarah Beth?" Mr. Fletcher yelled. "Child, are you breathing?"

I was too stunned to answer him.

Mr. Fletcher scrambled down the bank. I was ashamed of running off the road and scratching up my bicycle. He knelt down and put his hand on my back. "Sarah, can you hear me?"

I nodded yes.

"That's good," Mr. Fletcher said. "What hurts? Can you move your arms and legs?"

I could, but not without wincing. "My elbows hurt." Then I flexed my knees. "Ohhh, my knees hurt too."

"Bet so. Your kneecaps are scraped raw."

Mr. Fletcher took off his cap and twisted it in his hands. "Should I take you to the emergency room?"

"Nooo," I wailed. "I don't need an emergency room. I need to go home!"

Granny filled the sink with warm, soapy water. She cleaned my knees with a soft washcloth, then dabbed Merthiolate on them.

"Ah, that burns!" I squirmed on the toilet seat, as the medicine turned my knees an orangey red.

Granny blew cool air on them to stop the burning. While she was applying the bandages, Granny said, "Sarah Beth, what happened? Hiram said he tooted his horn to make sure you didn't pull out in front of him, and the next thing he knew, you were flying over the handlebars."

I shuddered. "The horn scared me." What I didn't say was that I had been afraid the truck would hit me, the same way the car had hit Robin.

That night I had trouble getting to sleep, and when I finally did, the bad dreams started. The black car sped down the street. I opened my mouth to scream, but no sound came out. When I ran toward Robin, the car hit both of us. I was falling, falling, falling, and then the car turned into a casket.

Granny switched on the light and hurried over to my bed. "Wake up, pumpkin. It's only a bad dream."

My heart raced. Though I wasn't sure if God was listening, I bowed my head and asked him to help me. I figured it couldn't hurt to ask.

I spent the next morning in front of the television, not really watching the shows, but glad for the noise.

Granny called to me from the kitchen. "Get your recipe box. I'm gonna teach you to make stewed potatoes."

While I peeled potatoes, Granny fried out fatback meat on the stove. "We have to keep busy," she said. "That'll make the waiting easier."

Keeping busy helped, but nothing could make waiting easy.

Next Granny had me use the cutting board and slice the potatoes into chunks. "Now drop them in the pot and cover them with water," she said. "Once they cook up nice and soft, we'll add thickening to them."

I flexed my sore knees. "What's thickening?"

"That's when you mix flour with a little water and form a paste," Granny said. "Then you add some milk. Thickening makes potatoes and corn creamier."

I wrote the recipe for the potatoes on a card and put it in my box.

Granny opened a new sack of flour and refilled the bin. "Sarah, go ahead and make some biscuits. They'll be good with the potatoes."

In a large bowl, I mixed flour, lard, and buttermilk. I found my rhythm working the dough and started humming one of Ruby's songs. Just as I was placing the last biscuit into the long, greased pan, the telephone clanged.

Chapter Eight

This Old House

Granny hobbled toward the den to answer the phone. A sick feeling washed over me, and I was afraid to move.

"What?" Granny said.

I grabbed the counter to brace for bad news.

"Does Charlie know? When did it happen?"

My stomach churned, and puke rose up in my throat.

"Sarah, come quick," Granny yelled. "Your mama needs to talk to you."

I stumbled to the telephone, and my legs gave out. Sinking into the green armchair, I put the receiver to my ear. "Mama, Mama, what's wrong?"

"Sarah, I didn't mean to scare you. Robin's awake!"

"Really?"

"Yes!"

"How . . . how did it happen?"

"I was reading a Billy and Blaze book to her, and when I got to the part about Billy getting a pony for his birthday, she opened her eyes! It was as simple as that." Some of the excitement left Mama's voice. "The doctors are examining her now."

The change in Mama's tone made me cautious. "Why are they examining her?"

The silence on the other end of the line lengthened. "They're checking for brain damage," Mama said. "But there's no need to borrow trouble. She's awake. Let's focus on that."

But I couldn't just focus on that. Brain damage could be almost as bad as dying! I handed the phone back to Granny. I ran out the back door and climbed my favorite oak tree. I found the spot where three branches met and cuddled up there. Tears nearly blinded me. There was only one thing left to do. I would become such a perfect big sister that I would make up for the accident. I started keeping a list inside my head. I'd read to Robin, tell her stories, play with her, and protect her from bullies. Maybe if I was absolutely perfect, it would make up for what happened. Maybe nobody would ever have to know the real truth.

Later that afternoon, Dad showed up for a visit. "Now that Robin's doing a little better, I wanted to see my other best girl. It's been a tough week for all of us."

He gave me a little smile, and that eased the sick feeling in my stomach.

"Sit, sit," Granny said. "How about a plate of stewed potatoes and some hot biscuits? Sarah's turning into a first-rate cook."

"That sure sounds good," Dad said. "I haven't had much of an appetite, but now that Robin's awake, I'm nearly starved."

"How is she?" I asked.

"Pretty good," Dad said. "She doesn't seem to remember the accident at all, but she knows her name, told the doctor she's six years old and that her favorite TV show is *Gunsmoke*."

If Robin didn't remember the accident, then she couldn't tell about me not paying attention. But why couldn't she remember? That bothered me a whole lot.

Dad attacked his potatoes like he'd been through one of Pharaoh's famines in the Bible. He even wiped his plate clean with a biscuit. "How about seconds?" he asked.

Granny refilled his plate, and he shoveled that down too.

I waited until Dad had pushed his chair back from the table. "How about Robin's leg?" I asked.

Dad's shoulders slumped.

Answer me, I thought. *Just tell me the truth.*

Instead, he looked up at Granny. "Maybe I should take Sarah Beth for a walk."

I followed Dad on the rocky path toward the tobacco barns. He had his head down and his hands jammed into his pockets. "Hey, daddy long legs," I called. Robin and me had nicknamed him cause he walked too fast for us to keep up.

He slowed down. "Sorry. I do my best thinking when I'm moving."

Finally, Dad stopped in front of Uncle John's house. It had been empty ever since he died. Dad sat down on the porch steps. He motioned for me to sit down too. "Nobody knows for sure about Robin's leg. The doctors say it's a blessing that she's so young. Young bones heal better than old ones."

"That's good news," I said.

Dad nodded. "But here's the tough part. She's gonna be in the hospital for several weeks and, when she gets out, she'll be coming home in a body cast. Do you know what that means?"

I shook my head.

"Robin will be flat on her back. One of us will have to feed her. She'll have to use a bedpan. She'll be about as helpless as a newborn baby."

Tears welled up in my eyes. "Robin likes to run and jump and climb."

"I know," Dad said. "That's why this will be a hard summer for her." He raked his hands through his Elvis Presley hair. "Once her cast comes off, she'll have to go back to the hospital for physical therapy. She'll probably walk with crutches for a while. Maybe even have a brace and special shoes."

I didn't say it out loud, but I worried other kids would make fun of a brace and special shoes. Thinking about that made me want to hit somebody.

"We're gonna be faced with a lot of medical bills," Dad said. "That's why your mama and I think we need to sell our house in town."

"Are you kidding?"

Dad shook his head no.

I couldn't believe what he had just said. "But it's our home. Where would we live?"

"Here," Dad said, gesturing toward the rundown house. "We have a mortgage in town, but Grandpa inherited this place. He's willing to let us live here for free."

I didn't want to move to the farm. I didn't want to be the new kid in school and live far away from the library and the town pool. I didn't want to give up my lavender library. "Do we have to?" I asked.

"I don't see any other way," Dad said. "Sarah Beth, I'm as sorry as I can be about all of this."

That made two of us.

Granny was waiting for me in the kitchen. "How did the talk with your daddy go?"

I shrugged.

"I know moving will be hard," Granny said.

I didn't want to talk about moving. I wanted to pretend it wouldn't happen. I pointed to the mixer, box of cocoa, and other stuff lined up on the counter. "What are you making?"

Granny smiled. "I thought I'd teach you to make a chocolate pound cake. We can take it to the hospital and pay Robin a visit. What do you think about having a little party to celebrate her waking up?"

For the first time all day, I smiled too.

Grandpa circled the parking lot, but there were no empty spots near the hospital entrance.

"Please hurry up!" I begged.

"Just be patient a little longer," Grandpa said. "You know I have to park near the front door so your granny won't have far to walk."

We made a second loop around the lot, and finally on the third time found a parking space.

As soon as Grandpa turned off the ignition, I scrambled out of the truck and raced through the parking lot.

"Slow down," Granny called. "You're walking too fast for my bad leg."

I tapped my foot on the pavement until they caught up.

Once inside, Granny stopped by the front desk to check the room number. Now that Robin was awake, the doctors had moved her to the third floor.

The elevator moved slow, slower than molasses stuck to the jar and only coming out in a trickle. When it finally stopped on the third floor, I pushed past the pokey nurses and headed down the hall.

"Be careful with the cake," Granny ordered.

I stood outside Robin's door with my heart slamming against my chest. It bothered me that she couldn't remember the accident. I had to see for myself that being in a coma hadn't changed her. That she still remembered me.

After all my hurrying, I couldn't make myself knock on the door. Granny did it for me.

Mama answered. "Come in! We've been waiting for you."

I handed the cake box to her and shot past the pile of stuffed animals and balloons straight over to Robin. Her bandaged leg still hung from a sling. The rails around her bed were like the bars on a jail cell.

Mama said in a matter-of-fact voice, "Being in traction will stretch Robin's muscles and tendons to help her heal."

"Can I hug her?" I wanted to be sure it was okay.

Robin held up her arms and I bent down. I closed my eyes and felt her soft skin. I took a deep breath, sucking in the smells of soap and baby lotion.

I would probably have hugged her forever, but she started to squirm. "Did you see all my presents?"

Her room looked like a Western toy store. It was filled with cowboy stuff, horse books, puzzles, stuffed horses, model horses, a wooden stable, even a pair of chaps.

"Where did it all come from?" I asked. "It's not even Christmas."

Mama threw her arms open wide. "From all over! Neighbors, church people, customers at your dad's service station, and some people that just read about her in the newspaper. Everybody has been so kind to us. We're blessed to live in such a good community."

"Who sent the chaps?" I asked.

"Cathy," Robin said. "They're my best present." She pointed at the Tupperware container. "What's in there?"

"Chocolate cake," Granny answered. "I've been teaching Sarah to bake."

Grandpa reached into the party bag he had brought from the car. He put on a triangle-shaped paper hat and blew on a kazoo.

"Would you act your age?" Granny asked.

Instead, he slipped a hat on her head and pestered me into wearing one too.

Mama pulled a hospital tray over and fed Robin a big bite of cake with lots of icing.

"You have a chocolate mustache," I teased.

"The cake is delicious," Mama said. "Maybe you should try for a ribbon at the county fair."

Robin stuck her tongue out and licked icing off her lips. "Sarah is good at everything," she said.

I looked at Robin's bandaged head. I stared at her leg hanging in a sling. I knew one thing that I was not good at. I was not a good babysitter.

"Why is Sarah crying?" Robin asked.

"Those are happy tears," Mama said. "Sarah is just so glad you're getting better."

Robin didn't seem to have brain damage, and I was happy as could be about that, but her leg worried me. I wanted her to be able to run and jump and play. I wouldn't feel better until she could.

Chapter Nine

Ruby Lee

Uncle John had built his house from a Sears Roebuck mail-order kit. Nobody had lived in it for a while, and it showed. The windows were grimy, the inside was dusty, and the whole place needed a good coat of paint.

"We have three weeks until Robin comes home," Granny said, "and it's canning time too. I'll be busy with Miss Irene, putting up the beans and tomatoes. How would you and Ruby Lee like a little project?"

I always loved spending time with Ruby. "What kind of project?"

"Clean this place up," Granny said, "and plant some flowers. Ruby sure has a way with gardening. Guess she inherited Miss Irene's green thumb."

I remembered my promise to be a perfect big sister. This was my first chance to prove it.

Granny took a closer look at the walls. "We'll pick up some paint chips at the hardware store and let your mama choose the colors."

At dawn, the smell of coffee mingled with sizzling country ham. I was still finishing breakfast when Ruby Lee knocked on the back door.

"Come on in," Granny called. "Can I fix you a biscuit?"

"No, ma'am. I had breakfast at home."

Granny wrapped up the leftover ham biscuits, and put them in a basket with slices of cake and a thermos of tea. "Thought you girls might enjoy having a picnic lunch," she said.

Ruby followed me outside to load Grandpa's truck. She raised her arm and pointed at the sky. "Look up yonder," she said.

The sky was streaked with pink, like God had used my crayons to color it. Ruby and me had watched the sun rise lots of times together. Tobacco priming started early. "It sure is beautiful, Ruby Lee." I placed a box of cleaning supplies into the truck and slid it toward the back.

Rowdy walked over and sniffed Ruby's hand. He wagged his tail and panted with his tongue hanging out.

Ruby ruffled his fur. "This here dog is a good judge of character," she said.

I giggled. "That's because he goes to church."

Rowdy jumped into the back of the truck and nestled beside the cleaning supplies. Ruby and I climbed into the cab with the picnic basket between us.

I shifted into drive and the old truck bumped along the worn path. "I'm glad for this job," Ruby said. "Your granny's paying me real good. I'm saving for back-to-school clothes."

My hands tightened on the steering wheel. I didn't want to think about changing schools. "I'll be the new kid."

"Ease up on that steering wheel," Ruby said. "Looks like you're trying to choke it." Ruby stared out the window. "Don't sweat school," she said. "Instead of worrying about one skinny white girl, folks will be whispering about integration, about all us uppity colored children drinking from the same water fountain, eating in the same cafeteria, and using the same bathrooms."

Instead of easing up on the steering wheel, I clenched my jaw too. I felt guilty that Ruby couldn't swim in the town pool or have a hamburger at Bubba's Grill. Sometimes grown-ups made stupid rules and were slow to change them, especially in Shady Creek. "Guess you're right," I said. "Going back to school will stink for both of us."

"It won't exactly stink for me," Ruby said. "I'll be going to a nicer school, one with real playground equipment." She wrinkled her nose. "But it will be hard. It's hard to go where you're not wanted."

When Ruby talked like that, I didn't know what to say. I wanted to fix things, but didn't know how.

I rolled the truck to a stop near the front porch. Ruby Lee climbed out and walked around the overgrown yard. "Somebody needs to mow the grass," she said. "Ask your grandpa if he wants Uncle Clarence to do it."

Ruby Lee unloaded the cleaning supplies while I unlocked the front door. "Come on and have a look," I said.

Ruby walked through the entire house: kitchen, dining room, den, two bedrooms, and a bath.

"I know the stove and refrigerator are old, and the tile is cracked. It's not nearly as nice as our house in town."

Ruby shrugged. "I know lots of people that live in worse. It won't seem so bad when it's clean and painted." She pulled a pencil and paper from her pocket.

"I'm gonna make us a list," she said. "This here is a big job."

While Ruby took notes, I opened all the windows to air out the house. "Here's the way I see it," Ruby said. "I'll start by scrubbing the bathroom. I can't stand a filthy bathroom."

I grabbed the mop handle and put a clean rag over the head. "I'll wipe down the walls and trim," I said. "Get rid of all the dust and cobwebs."

"And when you finish with that, the floors need a good sweeping," Ruby said.

I rolled my eyes behind her back. Sometimes Ruby thought she was the boss of me.

I spent the morning cleaning the walls and floors. The whole time, Ruby Lee sang in the bathroom.

My arms are tired, Lord
Gotta sweep the floors
Give me strength, Lord
To finish my chores.

I liked listening to Ruby. She had been named for a famous actress. Maybe that was why she loved to perform.

At lunchtime, we sank down on the front-porch steps with the picnic basket. I poured each of us a glass of sweet tea.

"Your granny sure knows how to make good iced tea," Ruby said. "Tastes just like Ma Rene's, full of sugar."

I unwrapped ham biscuits, and we munched in silence for a while. "This place feels peaceful," Ruby said. "The people that used to live here were happy folks. I can always tell that about a place."

I knew what Ruby meant. This house was like opening a box of underwear on Christmas morning. It wasn't a present I would have picked out, but I'd put it to good use anyway.

We finished up our biscuits, and then unwrapped slices of cake. "Prune cake," I said. "It's my favorite."

Ruby Lee arched her eyebrows. "I don't know about eating prunes," she said.

"Prunes are moist and sweet. But if you're too stubborn to try it, that's more cake for me."

Ruby sniffed and took a tiny taste. Then she took a bigger one. "I have seen the light," she said. "Nothing wrong with prune cake."

After lunch, Ruby and I started work in the kitchen. Ruby wiped out the cabinets while I scrubbed the oven.

Ruby started to sing.

Sorrow's overwhelmin' me
Hidden deep where no one sees
Sorrow's overwhelmin' me
Lord, show me how to set it free.

I knew Ruby was singing about her own parents, but the words seemed like they were written especially for me. I wondered how to set a sorrow free. It seemed like there should be a recipe for it.

"Why you doing battle with that oven?" Ruby asked. "Gonna wear yourself out." She walked over and took the steel-wool pad from my hand. Ruby moved the pad in a firm, circular motion. "See? Like this. Girl, why you all teary eyed? What's your problem?"

I shook my head.

"Robin is awake," Ruby said. "Chattering like a chip-munk is what your granny said. So why you all knotted up?"

I shook my head again.

Ruby handed the steel-wool pad back to me. "Suit yourself, then."

I went back to scrubbing, and Ruby measured for shelf paper.

"It was my fault," I blurted out.

Ruby kept cutting the paper in a straight line. She didn't even look up.

"I was supposed to be babysitting." My hands started to tremble. "Only I-I was reading my library book."

Ruby put down her scissors. She reached for me and then let her arms drop. When we were younger, we used to hug each other all the time, but not so much lately. All the talk about integration and the assassination of Martin Luther King had made us feel awkward about touching, like maybe we shouldn't.

"What do your parents say about it?" Ruby asked.

"I haven't told them. I haven't told anybody, except for you."

"Why not?"

I took a couple of deep breaths, in and out, in and out. "I'm afraid. Afraid they won't love me anymore."

Ruby snorted. "Sarah Beth Willis, that is crazy talk. Your parents love you the same way Ma Rene and Uncle Clarence love me. Forever."

"Maybe, but I don't want them to know. Promise you won't tell."

Ruby walked over to me and held out her finger for a pinkie swear. The way she used to do when we were little. "I promise," she said.

Chapter Ten

Broken Promises

Mama chose paint the color of sunshine for the walls in our house. Grandpa and Clarence did most of the painting. Ruby and I helped with the trim.

When we were all finished, Ruby placed a big pot of red geraniums near the front door. "Hard to be miserable in a house with yellow walls and pretty flowers," she said. "Cheer up, Sarah."

But that was easy for her to say. She wasn't the one whose sister was hurt.

Grandpa was waiting in the truck to take Ruby and me into town. Mama and Dad had packed up most of the household stuff, but I wanted to pack the lavender library myself. Ruby was gonna help me.

I knew the route from Grandpa's farm to our house in town by heart: Shady Creek Road onto Tucker, Main Street to North Maple Avenue, then left onto Walnut Circle. I gripped the seat's edge with both hands. This would probably be the last time that I'd ever be inside my old room.

After Grandpa shifted into park, Ruby and I climbed out of the truck. While Grandpa went to unlock the front door, I studied the skid marks in the street. I could hear the brakes and smell the burning rubber. It seemed so real, like it was happening all over again.

"Sarah." Ruby tugged on my arm. "Your grandpa's waiting on us."

I shivered, trying to shake off the bad memories. Maybe it was a good thing we were moving away from there.

Mama and Dad had been busy. The house was full of boxes, and the curtains were drawn. My life would never be the same. Not ever. I left Ruby and walked from room to room. Every part of the house brought back a good memory. I pictured Dad flipping buttermilk pancakes on Saturday mornings. "How many can you eat, Sarah Beth?" Robin's rocking horse still sat in her bedroom. I touched his yarn mane, and then set the horse rocking with my foot. I saved the lavender library for last. I thought about Mama tucking me in at night. I moved across the floor to the bookshelves and ran my fingers over my novel collection. Laura Ingalls, Ramona Quimby, Jo, Beth, Meg, and Amy. Some of my best friends were in these books.

When I turned around, Ruby was watching me from the hallway. She walked in and stood beside me. "You know what Ma Rene always tells me when I'm sad about my mama moving to Chicago?"

"No."

"She says, 'I can't stop it from hurting, Ruby Lee, but I'm right here. Hold on to me.'"

I reached for Ruby's hand. I hadn't done that in a long time. I stood still as pond water and remembered all the times Ruby and I had played together on the farm: climbing trees, wading in the creek, swinging on the old tire swing. I hoped she would always be my friend, that integration wouldn't mess that up. "Do you think we can be friends at school?" I asked.

Ruby's brown eyes looked old and sad. "No," she said, "not at school. Things are bound to change between us. We'll probably end up just like our grannies, only working together."

"But our grannies are friends."

Ruby shook her head. "No, they're not. My granny does whatever yours says. Real friends are equals."

I knew Ruby was just being honest, but lots of people were trying to change things. I'd seen it on the evening news. "When school starts back, maybe we should try and be friends. You know, be brave, like the Freedom Riders you told me about."

"We're not old enough to change things," Ruby said. But then a big smile spread across her face. "Maybe we could be friends at school. Wouldn't that be something? Maybe I'm not dreaming big enough."

While I was helping Granny wash up the supper dishes, Miss Irene yelled through the screen door. "Miss Maybelle, Miss Maybelle, you at home?"

"No peace around here," Granny said. "Wonder what's got Miss Irene so riled up?" Granny dried her hands on a dishtowel and went to answer the door.

Miss Irene and Ruby Lee followed her into the kitchen. "Have a seat," Granny said. "How about some sweet tea?"

Miss Irene shook her head no. "This ain't no social call. Sarah Beth is filling Ruby's head full of grand ideas."

"What?" I knew better than to interrupt a grown-up, but I couldn't keep quiet. "Ruby, what did I do?"

Ruby rubbed the back of her neck. "I told her we want

to be friends at school. That we're gonna be brave like the Freedom Riders."

"Heaven help us," Granny said. She sat down at the table. "I don't think you girls know what you're saying."

Miss Irene sat down across from Granny. "Praise Jesus," she said. "Maybelle, I need you to help me set these girls straight. I done lost Ruby's daddy. My nerves can't take no more upset."

Granny took off her glasses and polished them on her apron, a sure sign she was thinking hard. "Sarah, are you ready to be called bad names? How you gonna feel when Betsy Carter doesn't invite you to her birthday party? Or when you're not welcome at the lunch table?"

"But—"

Miss Irene held up her hand and cut me off. "Now it's my turn. Ruby Lee, you better mind your place. The colored children will call you uppity, and the white children will treat you like something bad they stepped in." Miss Irene looked at me. "Sarah Beth, you have a good heart, but if you can't even tell about the accident, where you gon' find the courage to stand up for Ruby Lee?"

Ruby gasped and her eyes got big and wide. She'd done broke our pinky swear and told Miss Irene my secret. It was written on her face plain as day.

I shook like Mr. Fletcher when he has one of his fits.

"That's enough!" Granny said. "Look at how Sarah's trembling."

Ruby ran out the back door, and Miss Irene smoothed her housedress over her knees. "I didn't mean to hurt nobody's feelings," she said. "I was just remembering how you told me Sarah wouldn't talk about the accident. That's all."

Granny leaned in close to Miss Irene. "I know you're afraid for your granddaughter, but I won't have you upsetting mine. You hear?"

Granny's voice was stern, and Miss Irene hung her head. She needed the milk and eggs from our farm. That was a powerful hold to have on somebody.

“I didn’t mean no harm,” she said.

I hung my head just like Miss Irene. I had never heard my granny use that tone of voice before, and I knew I was the cause of it. She was trying to protect me from my own wrongdoings.

Chapter Eleven

Storytelling

On the day of Robin's homecoming, I stood on a chair and tied a sign between two of the front-porch pillars. It said, WELCOME HOME ROBIN.

"It looks good," Ruby said.

I was surprised to see her standing in my yard. Granny and Miss Irene still worked together like nothing had happened, but since that day in Granny's kitchen, Ruby and me had been avoiding each other.

She held out a pie plate. "Ma Rene baked a peach cobbler for Robin's homecoming."

My mouth started to water. Miss Irene had a way with

pies. "That was nice of her. You can leave it in the kitchen with Granny."

After Ruby dropped off the pie, she helped me tie balloons to the porch railing. "We need to talk," she said.

I pointed to the open window. I didn't want Granny listening in. "Let's take a walk in the woods." We didn't go far, just out of earshot of the grown-ups.

"I blabbed your secret for a good reason," Ruby said. "It's too big to keep. If you won't tell your parents, you should at least talk to your granny about it."

"Are you apologizing?"

"No, I'm telling you the gospel truth."

Ruby owed me an apology. I stopped walking and crossed my arms. "You broke a pinkie swear, so I don't trust you anymore. That's the same as lying."

"It is NOT the same as lying," Ruby said. She put her hands on her hips. "Here's a newsflash: I don't trust you either. You may talk big, but you still eat at Bubba's Grill and swim in the town pool. You don't stand up for what's right. No wonder you're lying to your parents. Covering up IS the same as lying."

"Ah!" I touched my cheek. It hurt as much as if Ruby had slapped me. "Ruby Lee Kimmer, you're mean and hateful. And you're not my best friend anymore either!"

Ruby shook her fist at the sky. "I don't know why I listened to you in the first place. I knew we couldn't be friends at school." Ruby tossed her head. "Sarah Beth Willis, you ain't my best friend either. Fact is you're more like a chicken than a Freedom Rider!"

"You take that back!"

Instead, Ruby put her hands underneath her arms and flapped them like wings. She circled around me making chicken noises. "Bawk, bawk, bawk, bawk, bawk!"

"Stop it! Stop making fun of me!"

Ruby *bawk*ed even louder.

All the guilt and fear spewed out of me like a flash flood. "I hate you, Ruby Lee Kimmer. You're a—" And then I called her the most vile name I could think of. A name I knew Ruby hated. A word intended to make her people feel like dirt.

Ruby stopped *bawk*ing.

The look on her face made my chest feel tight. She had tears in her eyes, but looked as fierce as a warrior. "You are a racist," she said.

"I . . . I . . . I didn't mean it. You just made me so mad. All I wanted was for you to shut up."

"Some words can't be taken back," Ruby said. "Nobody is born a racist, at least that's what Ma Rene says. She'll see a little white baby and say, 'Look, ain't it precious, but before that baby is full-grown, its heart will be full of hate.' Guess that's what's happening to you."

"No!" I wailed. "I just got mad and said something stupid. Hasn't that ever happened to you? What about the time you told Ma Rene you hated her?"

"It's not the same," Ruby said. "You're white trash and don't have no room to be calling names. Don't you ever speak to me again. You hear?"

I was so rattled that I couldn't even think of a reply.

After Ruby stomped off, I yelled, "Get off our land and don't come back!" Ruby turned around and put the stink eye on me, but she didn't say any more. We'd been friends since we were babies, but it only took five minutes to blow that friendship to smithereens. Some words are like a stick of dynamite.

Granny opened the screen door and joined me on the porch. "Why such a glum face?"

I was still ashamed over my fight with Ruby, but I didn't want to ruin Robin's homecoming. "What is taking them so long to get here?" I asked.

"I don't know," Granny said. She shielded her eyes from the sun. "A watched pot never boils. Why don't you help me in the kitchen?"

I would have rather kept watch, but I followed Granny into the house. I started making biscuits, sifting the flour and working in the lard.

Granny put the chicken breasts, thighs, and legs in a cast-iron skillet full of hot grease. "After you finish the biscuits, you can help me make thickening for the gravy. It'll be good practice."

I made a well in the sifted flour and poured in some buttermilk. "Do you think Robin will ever be just like before?" I asked. "Able to run and jump?"

"Is that what's been bothering you?"

"Yeah, and a few other things."

"I reckon a big girl like you is asking for the truth," Granny said. "And the truth of it is nobody knows for sure. Not even the doctors." Granny wiped flour off the countertops. "All we can do is take good care of her and try to keep her spirits up."

While I finished the biscuits, I thought about Robin and Ruby. I would find a way to keep Robin's spirits up. Maybe if I thought of the perfect way, she would get well, but I wasn't sure what to do about Ruby. She made me mad enough to spit nails.

The meal was almost ready when Rowdy started barking. I ran onto the front porch and gripped the railing.

Dad and Grandpa carried Robin between them. Her cast started underneath her arms and covered her chest. A pair of makeshift shorts with snaps on the side hid her private parts. And then the cast fit over her legs. On the right side, only her toes were peeking out. On the left, the cast stopped just below her knee.

Sweat trickled down my neck. Robin must have been about to roast in that big plaster cast. Our little house didn't have air-conditioning either. That would make it even worse.

Robin didn't sleep well on her first night back home, and since we shared a room, I couldn't sleep either.

"Itches," Robin said. "It itches inside my cast."

My legs and arms started itching too. I clawed them with my fingernails. "I'm sorry," I whispered in the dark. "What about if I tell you a Billy and Blaze story?"

"No," Robin whispered back. "Make up a story. Make up a story about me."

I thought for a minute. "Okay, this story is about the Fourth of July Parade. Robin wanted to be in the parade, but she didn't play an instrument or know how to twirl a baton. She really wanted to ride a horse in the parade, but she didn't own one."

"Someday I will," Robin said.

I racked my brain for what might happen next. Figuring out the plot was always the hardest part. "Well, Robin was playing in Grandpa's barn. She saw the old hay wagon and had a great idea. She asked Grandpa to help her clean and paint it. That way they could hitch up the plow horses and drive the wagon in the parade."

"The horses' names are King and Nick," Robin said. "You should use their names."

"Okay. That way they could hitch up King and Nick."

"Did we decorate the wagon too?"

"Yep. With red, white, and blue crepe paper and balloons. The newspaper took a picture of Robin and

Grandpa, and they were on the front page. They were called 'Pioneer Stars'!"

"I like that story," Robin said, and pretty soon she fell asleep.

The next morning my arms and legs were covered in a red rash. The doctor said I had hives.

Chapter Twelve

Sarah's Great Idea

Mama slathered my arms and legs in a tan-colored lotion. "Now try not to scratch," she said.

I stared at myself in disgust. I looked as ugly on the outside as I felt on the inside. "Can I walk over to Granny's?"

"Sure," Mama said. "Go ahead."

Since the door was always unlocked, I let myself in. Granny was sitting in her recliner with her bad leg propped up. Every weekday at one, she fixed herself a glass of sweet tea and watched *All My Children*.

"What happened to your poor arms and legs?" Granny asked.

I sat down on the green vinyl couch. "Doctor Kern said I have hives."

"Bless your heart," Granny said. She lowered the foot-rest on her recliner. "Sarah Beth, run get the hairbrush and I'll braid your hair."

I sat on the floor in front of Granny while she brushed and braided. Granny kept her eyes fixed on the television. "That Erica Kane is mean as the devil," she said.

I liked *All My Children* too, especially the romance between Tara and Phil. "What did I miss?"

"Nothing," Granny said. "Sssh, now. It just started."

Granny got fighting mad when Erica tried to break up Tara and Phil. She said, "If I could get my hands on that Erica, I'd give her a good switching."

I knew Reverend Reece had told Granny watching soap operas was a sin, but she didn't care two hoots what he thought about it. Granny had told the reverend if her worst sin was enjoying a good story, she'd probably get to heaven before he did.

Granny kept brushing my hair, and I kept rooting for Tara and Phil. For a little while, my arms and legs didn't itch. I forgot what really happened on the day of the accident and about my fight with Ruby Lee. Granny and I loved a good soap opera.

On the walk back home, I thought about the story I had told Robin the night before. I looked at all the open land between Grandpa's house and Uncle John's. There was plenty of grass, and Grandpa had some extra fence posts in the barn.

When I got home, I settled down at the kitchen table with my journal and a copy of the *Tucker Post*. I circled an ad in the classifieds: "Pony for Sale Only $50."

Next I made a list:

1. *Plenty of pasture land.*
2. *Extra fence posts in Grandpa's barn.*
3. *Pony could stay at Grandpa's during the winter.*

4. *$25 left over from my birthday.*
5. *Granny and Grandpa could loan me the rest.*

A pony would be the perfect way to keep Robin's spirits up. All I had to do was convince my parents.

After Robin fell asleep for the night, Mama and Dad rocked on the porch swing.

I took my favorite spot on the steps. "Granny says we have to keep Robin's spirits up."

"You're good at that," Mama said. "I heard you telling her a story last night. Entertaining her is a big help."

"But I know a better way to help." I pulled the newspaper ad from my pocket. "Just like in the Billy and Blaze books, Robin wants a pony more than anything."

"As much as I'd like to buy her one, we can't afford it," Dad said.

Mama gasped. "Let me see that paper."

I picked up my journal. "The pony only costs fifty dollars. I have twenty-five dollars left over from my birthday, and Granny and Grandpa will pay for the rest." I hadn't asked them yet, but I knew they'd say yes.

"Absolutely not!" Mama said. "What if Robin were to get hurt again?"

Dad put his arm around Mama's shoulders. "Maybe we should think through this before we say no. We can't lock Robin away in a padded room." He pulled Mama a little closer to him. "Robin's got a hard row to hoe ahead of her, and a pony would give her something to look forward to."

"Having a pony would help her get well." I was sure of it.

Mama stood up and peeked inside to check on Robin. "Still asleep," she said. "I know the two of you are right about a pony making her happy, but I'm still too nervous."

Dad nodded. "Perfectly natural," he said. "But we've got to move past it."

Mama paced back and forth across the porch. "Being a parent is so hard," she said. "I should have been watching Robin instead of working in the garden. If I'd stayed close by, maybe this wouldn't have happened."

My hand flew to my mouth. Instead of blaming me, Mama blamed herself. A soft voice inside me whispered. *But it wasn't Mama's fault. It wasn't Mama's fault. It was mine.* I wanted to tell her the truth, I really did, but when I opened my mouth only a moan came out. "Aaaah." I started scratching my arms and legs.

"Stop that!" Mama scolded. "You'll cause those places to scar."

They itched so much I didn't care. Mama held out her hand. "Come on. I'll rub some more lotion on your hives."

"But can we get Robin a pony?" I begged.

"Stop pestering me," Mama said. "I already said no."

I tiptoed into the room I shared with Robin and climbed into bed. I wished I knew some way to change Mama's mind.

"Tell me a story," Robin whispered.

"You're supposed to be asleep."

"But I woke up. Now I want a story."

I was ready. I wanted to make the story even better by adding some more action in the middle. "Okay, after Grandpa and Robin decorated the wagon, they hitched up King and Nick. The wagon looked so pretty that Robin just knew they would win a blue ribbon, but then it started to rain. Rain fell like it was being poured from a bucket. Rain pounded against King and Nick."

"What about the decorations?" Robin asked.

"Ruined. The decorations were ruined."

"I don't like this story," Robin complained.

"Just wait, it'll get better. So thunder boomed. Rumble, roar, crash, crack! Lightning streaked across the sky. The storm scared King, and he jumped. Nick jumped too. It was a runaway wagon!"

"Then what happened?" Robin asked.

"Well, Grandpa was sawing on the reins, trying to get those horses under control, but he wasn't having much luck. Then Robin started talking to them. She shouted, 'Whoa, Nick. That's a good boy. It's all right now. Nothing to worry about. Whoa.' Those horses listened to Robin because she had always petted them and brought them carrots."

"I was their friend," Robin said.

"That's right. So King and Nick slowed to a trot. Finally, they slowed to a walk, and the sun came out as bright as a big lemon drop in the sky. Robin had saved the day!"

"That's one of your best stories," she whispered right before she fell asleep.

Chapter Thirteen

Potty Humor

On Saturday morning, Dad asked me to go for a drive. I was glad to have some time alone with him, but a little curious too.

"Dad, where are we going?"

He turned and winked at me. "I thought we'd go see that pony. There's no harm in looking."

I raised my fist in the air. But then I remembered how upset Mama had been. "Has Mama changed her mind?"

Dad waved at Mr. Carter, who rode by on his tractor. "She knows where we're going. If the pony is small and very gentle, maybe she'll consider it."

I crossed my fingers. Considering it might mean yes.

"Sarah Beth," Dad said, "I've been meaning to thank you and Ruby Lee for cleaning up the house. You girls did a fine job."

"Thanks." With the mention of Ruby Lee, my good mood flew right out the car window. Sometimes I was still mad at her, but mostly I was ashamed.

Dad laughed. "When I was about your age, Ruby's daddy used to help us prime tobacco. We'd race to see who could get to the end of the row the quickest."

I hardly remembered Ruby's daddy. He joined the army when we were little.

"I haven't seen much of Ruby this summer," Dad said. "Guess you girls are growing apart; that's what happened with Leon and me."

"Why?"

Dad's jaw tightened, and he looked straight ahead. "Separate schools, different friends. It was just easier that way, but I cried like a baby when he was killed in Vietnam. He was a good man."

It was too late for Dad and Leon to be friends again, but maybe not for Ruby and me. I needed to write her a letter.

Mr. Whitaker, who owned the pony, was wearing Wrangler jeans and a cowboy hat. We walked with him out to a red barn that was bigger than our house.

"Hey, Slim," Mr. Whitaker called. "The folks are here to see Butterball." A skinny cowboy led a pony out of the barn on a halter rope.

Butterball lived up to his name. He was as round as the cakes of butter from Granny's churning. I walked inside the riding ring to take a closer look at his brown and white spots. Butterball kicked up his back legs, but I was too quick for him.

"Sarah Beth, move outside the fence," Dad said sharply. He turned to Mr. Whitaker. "Why are you selling Butterball?"

Mr. Whitaker chewed on a piece of hay. "Well now,"

he said, "my granddaughter is an inexperienced rider. Ol' Butterball has a little too much spunk for her."

Mr. Whitaker kept talking about what a fine pony Butterball was, but I could tell Dad wasn't convinced.

Dad leaned against the riding ring, watching as Slim led Butterball around in a big circle.

Mr. Whitaker moved a little closer to Dad and said in a low voice, "It's a shame about 'em integrating Shady Creek. Guess your daughter will have to go to school with coloreds."

"Guess she will," Dad said. He kept his eyes on Butterball. "If I had my druthers, things would stay the same, but the law says different. I just hope no trouble comes to Shady Creek."

I scratched my head. Dad and Leon used to be like Ruby and me, but now he thought integration was a bad idea. Like most of the other grown-ups, he was afraid of change.

Dad stuck out his hand and shook Mr. Whitaker's. "I

appreciate your time, but Butterball is not what we're looking for. We need small and gentle."

I'd have to find another pony for Robin. I reached inside my shorts pocket and crumpled the newspaper ad.

Just before bedtime, I heard Mama crying on the porch swing. I closed the screen door and went to sit beside her. "What's wrong?"

Mama's dark eyes were swimming in tears. "Don't worry. I'm just feeling a little blue."

That answer didn't satisfy me one bit. "When you cry, I'm afraid about Robin."

Mama pulled a tissue from her pocket and wiped her eyes. "No, there's nothing new. It just hurts me to watch her suffer." Mama wadded the tissue in her hand. "I'd rather be in pain myself. I know you don't understand now, but someday when you're a mom, it'll make perfect sense to you."

I couldn't imagine being a mom. That would be in about a million years, but I did know how much it hurt to watch Robin suffer.

We rocked on the porch swing, and Mama's voice was soft, just above a whisper. "My shoulders ache from bending over the sewing machine." Mama was taking in some extra sewing to help make ends meet. "I miss having a dishwasher," she said, "and it's aggravating to live so far from town." Mama sighed. "Sorry to be such a complainer, but it *is* a beautiful night."

The lightning bugs were blinking in the dark while we glided back and forth on the swing. "What's going on with you and Ruby Lee?" Mama asked. "Every other summer, it's always been Ruby this and Ruby that."

"Nothing is going on. She's just busy." I wanted to tell Mama about my fight with Ruby and ask her at least a hundred questions about integration, but I was afraid of worrying her. As long as Robin was sick, I had to take a backseat. It felt sort of like I'd lost my parents. I didn't like it much, but that's the way it was.

Mama reached out and tucked a strand of hair behind my ear. "Don't look so serious. You're a beautiful girl when you smile."

I shook my head. "I'm not beautiful. I have too many freckles."

"Don't sell yourself short," Mama said. "You're a good writer, a kind person, and an attractive girl."

Mama was just trying to make me feel better. I wasn't cute and funny like Robin, or beautiful like Betsy, or musical like Ruby. I was just ordinary, and I wasn't nearly brave enough.

We kept rocking until Robin yelled, "I have to potty!"

Mama stopped the swing with her foot and wearily stood up. "I'd better hurry, or else I'll have to change the sheets too."

I followed Mama into the house.

"I hate the bedpan," Robin said. "My bottom feels dirty."

"Just finish," Mama said, "and then I'll clean your bottom."

Robin whimpered in frustration.

I said, "Hey, Rob, let's sing the stinky song."

Robin giggled and then sang along:

Diarrhea (sniff, sniff), diarrhea (sniff, sniff)
Some people think it's funny
But it's always black and runny
Diarrhea (sniff, sniff), diarrhea (sniff, sniff).

Mama finished cleaning Robin's bottom and emptied the bedpan. "You girls have a warped sense of humor," she said.

I thought a warped sense of humor was much better than an unhappy sister.

Chapter Fourteen

A Clean Slate

The next day, Robin threw her sketchbook on the den floor. "I'm tired of drawing."

"Want me to turn on the television for you?" I asked.

Robin shook her head no.

"I could read to you."

"I'm tired of listening."

"Well, stop complaining!" I yelled.

My arms and legs started to itch again. Robin was having a boring summer, and no matter how hard I tried to be a perfect big sister, I couldn't be one. Today wasn't the first time I'd yelled at her. I offered to bake some brownies to make up for it.

Robin stuck her bottom lip out and scowled. "Don't put any nuts in my brownies." Since she knew pecans were my favorite, nutless brownies were my payback for yelling.

I went into the kitchen and added an egg and some oil to the brownie mix. Then I threw in a big handful of pecans. I dipped a spoon into the batter for a little taste. "Ummm." I had a powerful urge to eat a whole spoonful. And then another one. I sat down on the kitchen floor with the bowl. I shoved spoonful after spoonful into my mouth. Even when I was full, I kept eating. I ate until it was all gone, and then I used my finger to clean every speck of icing from the empty bowl.

My stomach pooched out, and I felt like one of Grandpa's hogs being fattened for slaughter. I washed the dishes and mixed up another batch of brownies for Robin. This time without nuts.

"Sarah Beth," Mama called. "Something sure smells good."

I bent over double with stomach cramps.

Mama hurried across the kitchen floor. "What's wrong?"

"Stomachache."

Mama reached into the cabinet and found the terrible-tasting pink medicine. I had known all along the batter would upset my stomach, but I hadn't been able to stop eating it. In some strange way, punishing myself eased the guilt, at least a little.

Since Robin couldn't sit up, she had to eat her meals in bed. While Mama fed her, I got into the habit of sitting cross-legged by Robin's cot. Before long, the whole family was eating in the den.

One night after supper, Dad said, "We could all use a little cheering up. Mama and I have been talking about it, and we're gonna buy a pony, just as soon as we can find a really gentle one."

Robin clapped her hands together. Even her toes were twitching. "I wish we could get the pony right now!"

I had finally found a way to make Robin happy, but I still didn't know what to do about Ruby. We'd never stayed mad this long before.

"Fencing comes first," Mama said. "Starting tomorrow, Dad and Grandpa are gonna build a fence. That way the pony will have a place to run and play."

"He needs a barn too," Robin said.

Dad shook his head. "This winter the pony can stay at Grandpa's. Maybe we can afford a barn next year."

"I can't wait to have a real pony!" Robin said.

I felt the knot in my stomach ease. If Robin got well AND got a pony, maybe that would be enough to make up for the accident.

"Do you think Ruby would come see my pony?" Robin asked. "She hasn't been here all summer."

I guess Robin missed her too.

Using a posthole digger, Dad tunneled into the red dirt, making holes two inches deep and about eight inches apart. Then Drucker, Hiram Fletcher's grandson, filled the area around the post with dirt and tamped it down with a shovel. Sweat soaked through his light-blue shirt.

I pulled the curtain back and watched them work. Mostly I watched Drucker. He was really cute.

"Why do you keep looking out the window?" Robin asked.

"No special reason." I combed my hair and put on some Pink Passion lip gloss. "I'm gonna carry a pitcher of sweet tea outside. They're taking a break."

The muscles in Drucker's arms bulged. He was at least a head taller than me and had wavy brown hair.

"That tea hits the spot," Dad said. "How about a refill? Hellooo, Earth to Sarah."

"What? Oh . . . tea . . . sure."

"One of these days, I'm planning to build a barn," Dad

told Drucker. "I'd love to work on it now, but I need to wait because of Robin's medical bills."

Drucker held out his glass for a refill. I noticed his eyes were blue like the ocean. "If you need extra help, I'm good with a hammer," he said. "I'm saving to buy a minibike."

Dad wiped his face with a red bandana and sized up Drucker. "You're a hard worker, and you'll be even stronger by next year." He stuck out his hand. "Young man, you've got a deal."

Drucker shook Dad's hand and grinned. His teeth were white enough to be in a Colgate commercial.

I thought life in the country was looking up, until I noticed Drucker staring at my legs. I had hives again. Why couldn't I just be a normal girl with a normal crush? Instead, I had a sister in a body cast, an ex–best friend, and a bad case of hives. It was turning out to be the worst summer of my life.

The next morning I took the newspaper and went to see Grandpa. I wanted to ask him about a horse sale at the Tucker Stockyards.

"He's still doing up the morning chores," Granny said. "He'll be in directly. Why don't I make you some cinnamon toast while you wait on him?"

"Sounds good." Granny's cinnamon toast always filled the kitchen with a spicy, buttery scent. Just thinking about it made my mouth water.

"Why do you want to go to a smelly old livestock sale?" Granny asked.

"It's a horse sale, but it's held at the stockyard. Maybe we could find a pony there."

Granny added cinnamon, brown sugar, and a splash of vanilla flavoring to some softened butter. "I didn't think of that. Usually Grandpa buys cows when he goes to the stockyard."

I poured myself half a cup of coffee and filled the other half of the cup up with milk. "If we buy Robin a pony, it'll help her get well. Then I can forget all about the accident."

Granny spread the softened butter mixture onto the bread. "Pumpkin, that's not how it works. You can move past the accident, but you'll never forget it."

That was not the answer I wanted to hear. Like Ruby's song, I needed to find a way to let all the bad stuff go. "Granny, have you seen Ruby lately?"

"A few times. She's been busy practicing with the church choir."

"I had an argument with her, but I really miss her."

"About what?"

"Telling secrets and school integration."

Granny put the cinnamon toast in the oven. "Sarah Beth, there's a fine line between blacks and whites. School will be easier for you and Ruby if you don't try to cross over it."

I sat down at the table with my coffee. "I know it would be easier, but you've always told me just because something's easy don't make it right."

Granny frowned, like I was paining her. "I'm just trying to keep you safe," she said, "safe and happy."

I reckoned I was safe enough, but I sure wasn't happy.

While the cinnamon toast baked, Grandpa made his way into the kitchen and washed up. He sat down beside me at the table. "What you got there?" he asked, picking up the newspaper ad.

"A horse sale. Do you think they might have ponies?"

Grandpa took a closer look. "They just might. Let me talk to your dad about it. I've got twenty-five dollars just burning a hole in my pocket."

I bit into my cinnamon toast, but I didn't enjoy it as much as I usually did. I was thinking too much, about Ruby, and how Granny said I could never forget the accident. I needed to start over, like when I shook my Etch A Sketch and got a nice clean slate.

CHAPTER FIFTEEN

Surelick

On the day of the horse sale, Dad hitched a trailer to Mama's car, and the two of us made the drive to Tucker.

The stockyard was full of trucks and livestock trailers. The people headed into the auction wore Old Hickory overalls like Grandpa's, or jeans like Dad and me. The building had high ceilings and concrete floors. I wrinkled my nose at the smells of hay, leather, and manure.

We sat side by side on the bleachers, with a good view of the corral. On my left side sat a real cowboy. I kept sneaking glances at his hat, shiny belt buckle, and boots. He'd make a good character in a bedtime story for Robin.

The auctioneer talked at a fast clip. I didn't see how anybody could understand him.

The quarter horses were for sale first. "They're my favorite kind of riding horse," Dad said.

The cowboy agreed with him. "You can't beat a good quarter horse," he said. "I'm hoping to buy one today."

I looked at the program but didn't know what some of the words meant. "What's a Haflinger?"

"Haflingers are chestnut colored with a white mane and tail," Dad said. "Lot of people use them to pull wagons. Wouldn't mind owning one myself."

Since it would be a long time before the ponies, I went to the concession stand for a hot dog. I got in line behind two girls who looked about my age.

The tallest one said, "I wanted to cry when that man in the parking lot hit his pony with a whip."

The shorter girl shuddered. "No wonder the pony was afraid to leave the trailer."

I forgot all about buying a hot dog. I stepped in

front of the girls. "Do you remember what that pony looked like?"

The tall girl had friendly green eyes, like me. "Yeah, the pony's chestnut with a white mane and tail. He has the same coloring as a Haflinger."

"The owner's name is Granger," the other girl said. "His wife said, 'Granger, stop it. If you hurt that pony, he won't bring a fair price.' "

"Thanks. It sounds like that pony needs a good home."

I hurried back to my seat and scanned the program until I found the pony for sale by Granger Stevens. I pointed to the listing. "We should buy this one," I told Dad, and then I told him all the reasons why.

When we got our first glimpse of Mr. Stevens's pony, it broke my heart nearly in two. He had sad eyes and was way too skinny.

Dad frowned. "Looks like that pony has been nearly starved." He sighed. "Sarah Beth, maybe we should bid on a healthier one."

I used my pitiful face on him. "Please. He needs rescuing."

Dad started the bidding at twenty-five dollars.

"Got twenty-five dollars, twenty-five. Anybody give me thirty?" the auctioneer asked.

A woman in a Western shirt raised her hand.

"Please don't let her outbid us," I whispered. "Please, Dad."

"Got thirty dollars, thirty dollars. Anybody give me thirty-five?"

Dad nodded.

The bidding went back and forth between the woman and Dad. Thirty-five dollars, forty dollars, forty-five, fifty, fifty-five.

"Got fifty-five, fifty-five, fifty-five," the auctioneer chanted.

The woman in the Western shirt shook her head.

"Fifty-five going once! Fifty-five going twice!"

I bounced in my seat like a jumping bean.

"Sold to the man in the R. J. Reynolds cap," shouted the auctioneer.

I celebrated by throwing my program into the air!

Dad tipped his cap and grinned.

Dad led the chestnut-colored pony on a halter rope to our trailer, but the little pony balked and wouldn't walk onto the ramp.

"He's afraid because they whipped him."

Dad eyed the pony. "He sure likes you, Sarah. Turns his head every time you speak."

"He's about the same size as a large dog," I said. "Maybe we could put him in the back of the car, and I could talk to him all the way home."

"That's the craziest thing I've ever heard of," Dad said, but he was already opening the car's back door. Dad climbed in the front seat, knelt down facing the back, and pulled on the halter rope.

I talked to the no-name pony in a soft voice. "There's nothing to be afraid of. You're going home with us now." I petted him until he trusted me enough to scramble into the back, just the way I wanted him to.

The pony was calm on the way home. He rode with his head stuck out the window. I told him all about the farm. How he'd have plenty of grass, oats, and hay to eat, and a big pasture to explore. He snuffled like he understood me.

Dad kept looking in the rearview mirror. "I'd hate to hear your mama if we end up with a load of manure in the backseat of her car."

I didn't know how to keep that from happening, but I kept a watch on the pony's hind end, just in case. We were lucky, and he minded his manners.

Dad tooted on the horn as we headed up the driveway.

Mama, Granny, and Grandpa hurried out to the front porch to see what all the ruckus was about. "You're pulling a perfectly good trailer behind that car," Mama yelled. "What in the world is a pony doing in the back?"

Grandpa chuckled. "A better question might be how are we gonna get him out?"

"That's easy," Dad said. "All I need is a bucket of oats. It's been so long since this pony had enough to eat that he'd follow a bucket of oats about anywhere."

I couldn't wait for Robin to see her pony. I tugged on Dad's arm. "Can we move Robin's cot onto the porch?"

"That sounds like a good idea," he said. "Robin would probably enjoy a little fresh air."

Grandpa and Mama moved Robin onto the porch. Dad rattled the oats bucket, while I coaxed the pony toward the house. He stopped and eyed the steps.

"Come on, little fella," I said. "Only two steps." And with a final rattle of the oats bucket, the pony climbed up. His hooves clomped across the porch.

Robin's smile was big and wide, the way it used to be before the accident. I wished I could tell Ruby about it. She'd understand how good I felt, like when her mama sent a letter from Chicago.

Robin made a clicking sound by putting her tongue behind her teeth. "Come here, boy," she called. "*Click, click, click.*"

The pony's ears perked up, and he stopped beside Robin's bed and nuzzled her hand.

"What do you think?" I asked.

"I love him," Robin said. "He's beautiful."

The pony was much too skinny to be beautiful, but if Robin thought he was that was good enough for me.

"I want to take a ride," she said.

Mama's face scrunched up like she was trying hard not to cry. "I know you do, but you have to get the cast off first."

Robin scowled at Mama. "How many days until I'm all better?"

"We don't know for sure," Mama admitted.

Robin's face turned red.

This had been a good day so far. I didn't want it to be ruined. "Your pony needs a name, Rob. What are you gonna call him?"

The pony stood very still while she petted him. "His name is Surelick," she said.

I walked over and petted the pony too. "That's a funny name. Why are you calling him that?"

Robin pointed to the empty oats bucket in Dad's hand. "Because my pony is a good eater. He sure licked the bucket clean."

"I like it. It's an unusual name."

I kept watching Robin and Surelick. It was love at first sight, but would he really help her get well? I sure hoped so. I was running out of ideas.

After Dad turned Surelick out to pasture, Robin asked for her sketchbook.

Since Mama and Dad were both close by, I tucked my journal underneath my arm and went for a walk in the woods. Normally, I would've gone to Ruby's house, but not anymore. Sunshine sifted through the leaves, warming my face. I wasn't sure where the path led, but I wanted to find a private place to write a letter to Ruby.

I stepped over tangled vines, slid down a steep hill, and came to a clearing with a pond. I made my way closer to the boy sitting beside the water. His elbows rested on his bent knees, and his head drooped toward his chest.

"Drucker?"

I must have startled him. He jerked his head in my direction. "I wasn't expecting company."

My face felt like I had been sitting too close to a campfire. I held out my journal. "Sorry. I was looking for a private place to write. Our house is pretty tiny."

Drucker patted the ground beside him. "Don't let me scare you off. Have a seat."

I sat down and wrapped my arms around my knees. "I've never been here before."

"This is part of my grandpa's land," Drucker said. "That steep hill you just walked down is the boundary between your family's property and ours."

"Uh-oh, sounds like I'm trespassing."

Drucker gave me a lopsided smile. "Nobody cares about that. I'm the only company you'll ever meet out here, except for stray cows."

I patted my journal. "I was planning to write. What do you do out here by yourself?"

Drucker picked up a rock and scrambled to his feet. "I usually come here to skip stones. It helps me think." He held the rock between his thumb and fingers and threw it with an arcing motion, like a Frisbee.

I didn't have to ask what Drucker needed to think about. Just like everybody else in Shady Creek, I knew his parents were getting a divorce.

Drucker's rock bounced off the water six times before it sank. He picked up another rock and handed it to me. "Here, you try it."

My rock sank on the first try. Drucker stepped behind me and took my arm. He moved it back and forth. "You need a twenty-degree angle between the stone and water," he said.

I looked up at him. "Are you telling me there's a science to this?"

"There sure is," Drucker said, "and according to the *Guinness Book*, the record is fifty-one skips."

"How is that possible?"

"Beats the heck out of me," Drucker answered. "My personal best is ten skips." He let go of my arm and picked up some more rocks.

"My dad says you're the quarterback for the Shady Creek Cougars."

"Yeah, we should be pretty good this year. We picked up a star running back from the colored school."

Integration was everywhere, or so it seemed. "How's that working out? Having blacks and whites on the same team."

"Hard at first. We had a fight, but Coach broke it up."

"Did anybody get hurt?"

"Nah, a couple bloody noses is all. We're doing better now."

Drucker went back to skipping stones. I thought maybe he'd rather be by himself, since he quit talking to me. Anyway, I couldn't write with him standing so close by. It would be too weird. I picked up my journal from the ground. "I should get going."

Drucker threw another rock. "If you decide to trespass again, bring brownies. Your dad said you're a good cook."

I ducked my head. It sounded like Dad had been bragging about me. I wondered what else he had told Drucker. It was awful embarrassing!

Chapter Sixteen

Walking on the Moon

I leaned back against my bed and wrote *July 20, 1969*, in my journal. It was a special day. If everything went according to plan, Neil Armstrong and Buzz Aldrin would be the first men to ever step foot on the moon. The moon walk was even gonna be on television. I figured, like me, Ruby was planning to watch it. Nearly everybody was.

I had tried writing to Ruby about ten times, but I had never finished. I wasn't sure how to ask forgiveness for the unforgivable. Today would be the day though. My mind was made up about it.

Dear Ruby,

I'm lonely since we stopped being friends. The farm is not nearly as much fun without you. If I had a magic eraser, first I'd erase Robin's accident, and then I'd erase our fight. I'd especially erase the mean name I called you. I know you'll never forget what I said, but is there any way you could ever forgive me for it? I am really, really sorry.

Your ex-best friend,
Sarah Beth Willis

After I put the letter in the mailbox, I felt a whole lot better. It was like I'd been holding my breath underwater and could finally breathe. Ruby might never forgive me, but at least I was trying to make things right. If I didn't hear from her in a couple of weeks, I'd write to her again.

On my way back from the mailbox, I heard Mama calling my name. I hurried to the kitchen to see what she wanted. "I could use some help getting ready for Cathy's visit," Mama said.

Since Cathy was going away to college, she was bringing Scruffy to live with us on the farm. Robin and I were excited to finally have a dog of our own.

I set the table and filled water glasses while Mama made coleslaw for supper. "Cathy's late," Mama said. "I hope she didn't miss the turnoff."

"We need a sign to mark the turnoff. Grandpa said he's gonna paint one, but . . ."

Mama laughed. "I love your grandpa, but he's a big procrastinator. I won't hold my breath while he gets around to it."

Dad carried in a platter of hamburgers, hot off the grill. "Cathy is headed up the driveway," he said.

A few minutes later, Cathy hurried in, carrying Scruffy in one arm and a Samsonite overnight bag in the other. "Sorry I'm late. I think I turned beside the wrong cornfield." Cathy put Scruffy down, and he ran to find Robin. "Thanks for inviting me. It's too quiet without all of you next door. The couple that bought your old house doesn't have any kids."

I walked over to the window between the kitchen and den, and stared outside. The new owners had probably painted the lavender library a different color. I felt sick about my old room belonging to someone else.

In the den, Robin threw a plastic bone to Scruffy. Thud . . . thud . . . thud. He ran to fetch it, and then stood on his hind legs so she could take it from his mouth.

"I'm glad he's gonna live with us," she said. "He's a smart little dog."

Mama pulled a chair beside Robin's cot and cut up her hamburger with a fork. Cathy and I sat cross-legged on the floor to keep them company.

Cathy's eyes got misty every time she looked at Scruffy.

It must be hard to go away to college, like our move to the farm.

"I'd like to propose a change in plans," Mama said. "How about we share Scruffy? He can live with us while Cathy's away, and with her when she's home for breaks."

Cathy pressed her hand to her heart. "Could we do it that way, please?"

Robin and I agreed that would work just fine.

I carried my empty plate to the kitchen and helped Mama and Cathy with the cleanup. By the time we finished, Robin had fallen asleep.

"I'm glad she's napping," Mama said. "Otherwise she'd never stay up long enough to watch the moon walk."

Cathy and I decided to play checkers until it was time for it to start. She won the first match, and I double jumped with one of my kings to take the second one.

Robin woke from her nap screaming. "Help me," she cried. "It itches so bad inside my cast!"

She itched nearly every day, but this time seemed much worse. I ran over and knelt beside her bed. "Where does it itch?"

"My back," she cried. "Take the cast off!"

We had to help her! "What about a coat hanger?" I asked Dad. "You could straighten one out like when we roast marshmallows. That would be skinny enough to reach inside."

Dad shook his head. "The doctors said not to put anything inside her cast. We can't risk injuring her because there's no way to treat it."

"What about my fingers?"

"That just might work," Mama said. "Sarah's hands are tiny. I've always said she should be a piano player with those long, skinny fingers."

Dad bent down and talked to Robin. "I'm gonna turn you on your side. Don't worry. I won't drop you. Sarah is gonna be very gentle and slip her fingers inside your cast. She'll give your back a good scratching."

I slid my fingers underneath the top of the cast. I

moved them up and down, up and down, like a yo-yo. Then I scratched the other side.

Robin finally stopped fidgeting. "It's all better now," she said.

I pulled my fingers out, and Dad placed Robin on her back. "Hang in there," he said. "It won't be much longer now. Hopefully, they'll take your cast off in a couple of weeks."

Mama and Dad moved over to the couch. He put his arm around her, and she leaned her head on his shoulder. We were all miserable.

"Don't look so sad," Cathy whispered to me. "She won't have to wear the cast much longer. How about some popcorn? We can munch on it during the moon walk."

We dimmed the lights, poured Cokes, and made popcorn. It was a lot like watching a movie.

Robin yawned. It was almost eleven. Way past her bedtime. "I bet this won't be as good as *Gunsmoke*," she said.

"Sssh," I whispered. "We don't want to miss anything."

"I'm going to step off the LM now," Mr. Armstrong said. He wore a white, bulky suit with a helmet and touched the moon's surface. The dust was almost like powder. "That's one small step for a man, one giant leap for mankind," he said.

Dad whistled loudly, and the rest of us clapped. "Boy, that's something," Dad said. "Those men are all the way to the moon, and we can hear them right here in our living room!"

Mama kept sewing snaps on another pair of shorts for Robin. "I had my doubts, but it seems they've pulled it off."

The astronauts planted an American flag on the moon. I felt patriotic, like when I watched fireworks on the Fourth of July or heard the national anthem playing.

"Do you think ponies and dogs will ever walk on the moon?" Robin asked.

Cathy shook her head. "Nah, I don't think animals would like being inside those padded suits."

Robin crossed her arms. "The suits are better than my cast. The astronauts can still walk and jump."

I bit my fingernail clear down to the quick. I wanted Robin to walk and jump so much I could barely breathe. It was hard to believe that Buzz Aldrin and Neil Armstrong could walk on the moon, but Robin couldn't take a single step on Earth. It didn't seem fair.

Chapter Seventeen

Back to the Hospital

Robin pitched a fit when Mama put their suitcases by the front door. "I don't want to go back to the hospital," she yelled. "I hate it there!"

"It won't be like last time," Mama promised. "You'll only be in the hospital for a week of physical therapy."

Scruffy started howling along with Robin. I scooped him into my arms and knelt beside her cot. "I wish you didn't have to go, but you can't ride Surelick until they take the cast off."

Robin grabbed my free hand. "They're gonna saw it off. What if they cut me in two?"

I looked up at Mama. "How do they get her out of the cast? It won't hurt, will it?"

Mama made a time-out sign with her hands. "Girls, stop and listen. It's a special kind of saw that doesn't cut skin."

Robin's eyes darted between Mama and me. She squeezed my hand. "I tell you what," Mama said. "I'll have the doctor show you how the saw works. I won't let him start until you're completely comfortable with it. I promise."

"Cross your heart?" Robin asked.

Mama made a big X sign across her chest. "Cross my heart," she said.

After Dad loaded the suitcases, I held the screen door open for him and Grandpa to carry Robin to the car.

"Take care of Scruffy and Surelick," she said.

"I will. Don't worry."

Mama put her arm around my shoulders. "I'm sorry to leave you again, but your grandparents will take good care of you. Remind your granny about the Back-to-School Ice-Cream Social on Thursday."

I said okay, but just thinking about a new school made my arms and legs itch.

Dad tooted the horn, and Mama hurried down the steps. As the car pulled away, Grandpa was the only one waving. I jammed my hands in my pockets. What if the doctors couldn't fix Robin's leg? What would happen to my family then?

After supper at Granny and Grandpa's, I paced around the den. I was tired of worrying about Robin and bored without Ruby Lee. There was nobody to push me on the swing, or wade in the creek with.

"Walk outside with me," Granny said. "I could use some help watering the hydrangeas."

I followed Granny outside and filled up the watering cans with the garden hose.

"You're awful quiet," she said. "Are you worried about going to a new school?"

"Maybe a little bit."

"No need to be nervous. You already have friends."

I scuffed my sandal in the dirt. "I've been wondering about that. I know it'll be hard, but maybe I should make up with Ruby Lee."

Granny bent over and turned off the spigot. "Course you should make up with Ruby, but remember what me and Miss Irene told you about school. Times are changing, and we don't need trouble."

"I think times are barely changing."

"It seems that way because you're young," Granny said. She walked over by the front porch and pulled some dead leaves off one of the hydrangea bushes. "Time passes much faster when you get old. To Miss Irene and me it's a miracle that blacks and whites will be going to the same school. We never expected to see such as that."

I emptied the rest of my watering can on the last blue-flowered bush. "I miss Ruby. I wrote her a letter, but I don't know if she'll read it."

Granny squinted off into the distance. "I've been friends with Miss Irene nearly sixty years. If we were as stubborn as you and Ruby, no quilting or canning would ever get done."

"Ruby's as stubborn as an old mule."

Granny laughed. "You're just as stubborn as Ruby Lee. Why don't you call her and get it over with? One of you has to make the next move."

But the truth was, I was afraid to call Ruby. I needed the letter to soften her up first.

Back in the den, Grandpa snored in his brown reclining chair. His chin bobbed against his chest, and he sounded like a noisy freight train.

"We need a project to keep our hands busy," Granny

said. "If you'll get my sewing basket from the corner shelf, we'll make a surprise for Robin."

Granny's sewing basket was full of buttons and colored threads. I handed it to her, and she pulled a white pillowcase from the bottom. "How about sketching an outline of Surelick on here?"

I peered over Granny's shoulder. "Sure, I can do that. But what are you gonna do with it?"

Granny searched through her basket and chose a dark-brown embroidery thread. "We'll embroider around your sketch and make a special pillowcase for Robin. What do you think of this color?"

"No, not that one. It's too dark." I searched through the basket and picked a golden-brown thread.

"I believe you're right," Granny said. "The little fella is exactly the color of caramel candy."

I moved to the kitchen table and spread out the pillowcase. I got a clear picture of Surelick in my mind. I drew him cantering through the pasture, because Robin loved to run. If she could just get well enough to ride, maybe everything would turn out okay.

When I finished drawing, I carried the pillowcase to the den and showed Granny.

"That's darn near perfect," she said.

I pulled up a stool and Granny asked me to thread the needle. "I have trouble seeing close up," she said. "That's what happens when you're old as dirt." Granny took tiny stitches, pushing the needle through the fabric and poking it back through from the other side.

"Robin will love this," I said. "She wants a Western room."

Granny looked up from her embroidery. "You girls share a room. What do you want?"

I wanted something I couldn't have . . . the lavender library back. "I can't have what I want. There's no privacy when you share a room with your little sister."

"Reckon not," Granny said, "but we could sew up a nice quilt for your bed." She looked over at Grandpa.

"Bet he'll have a crick in his neck from sleeping in that chair."

I gave Grandpa a gentle shake on my way to bed. While I was putting on my flowered pajamas, the phone rang. I cracked the door open, just an inch, and listened to Granny.

"Don't worry about Sarah," she said. "We're looking after her. How's Robin?"

I put my ear closer to the door.

"I'm not surprised," Granny said. "Physical therapy sounds like hard work. I hate she's having so many problems. I really do." Granny was quiet for a while, and then she said, "Charlie, don't get discouraged. Robin will learn to walk again. The Bible says if you have faith the size of a mustard seed, you can move mountains."

I climbed into bed. I whispered, "Please help Robin learn to walk again. Please." I wondered about faith, mountains, and mustard seeds. I punched my pillow and flopped onto my back. I was still staring at the ceiling when the clock struck midnight. I wished I had Ruby to tell my troubles to. That would help a whole lot.

The next morning, Grandpa dropped me off at the library as soon as it opened. Mama and Dad were too busy with Robin to answer my questions, and Granny was stuck in the past. She and Miss Irene didn't want Ruby and me to be friends at school, but maybe they were wrong. Mrs. Brown, our librarian, had answered almost any question I'd ever had. She would tell me the truth.

I was the only customer except for Mr. Johnson, and since he was fast asleep, he didn't really count. I marched up to the checkout desk. "Mrs. Brown, do you have time to answer some questions?"

"Of course I do. On what topic?"

"School integration."

Mrs. Brown fiddled with the chain attached to her glasses. "Sarah Beth, you are always full of questions, but I didn't anticipate this one." She straightened her shift and smoothed the sides of her beehive hairdo. "For those with an inquisitive mind, there's no such thing as a boring day in the library. Come with me."

Mrs. Brown pulled a scrapbook from a locked file cabinet. We sat beside each other at one of the empty tables, and Mrs. Brown opened the book. "I've been saving newspaper and magazine articles about civil rights since *Brown versus Board of Education* back in '54."

I found out real quick that I'd been sheltered from most of the hatefulness. Mrs. Brown said, "In Arkansas, it took the National Guard to integrate Central High School."

"Do you think that'll happen in Shady Creek?"

She shook her head. "I don't believe so. It's been fifteen years since the Supreme Court ruled. We've watched all the violence unfold elsewhere, and the committee charged with school integration is working hard to avoid it. I'm on the committee, you know."

Mrs. Brown started to close the scrapbook, but I grabbed her hand. "Who's that?"

"Emmett Till," she said, "but I won't talk to you about him. One of your parents needs to accompany you to read about Emmett Till."

That made me want to know about him even more.

Mrs. Brown put the scrapbook back in the file cabinet and locked it. "In Shady Creek, we have blacks and whites working together, priming tobacco and pulling corn. Attending the same school won't be much different than that."

"Granny says if I try to be friends with coloreds, I'll be called names and left out of birthday parties."

"*Ostracized* is the word you're looking for," Mrs. Brown said. "Your granny could be right." She patted my hand. "I've given you a lot to think about, but should you decide to broaden your circle of friends, you'll have an unexpected ally. I have it on good authority that the new sixth-grade teacher at Shady Creek will be a Negro. A very intelligent, dignified woman. In fact, Mrs. Smyre will be stopping by here later to pick up some books."

Now I understood the things grown-ups whispered about, and why my mama was sometimes quick to turn off Walter Cronkite on the evening news. I thanked Mrs. Brown for answering my questions.

"No thanks are necessary. Answering questions is the best part of my job."

Mrs. Brown turned to leave, but I had one more question. "Where did the new teacher come from?"

"She used to teach at the colored school. The teachers from that school will be integrated in schools throughout the county, same as the students."

I sat in the library for a long time. I watched Mrs. Smyre stop by for her books. She was with a little girl who looked so much like her—same eyes and mouth—that I knew they were mother and daughter. The little girl giggled, and Mrs. Smyre put her finger to her lips. "Sssh." The teacher smiled and bent down to tie her daughter's shoe.

While I watched them, a big lump formed in my throat. I wondered if the little girl was nervous about being in a classroom full of white children. I wondered if it would seem strange to Mrs. Smyre to teach mostly white children, with only a dark face or two mingled in. I hoped the people in my town would be kind to them.

This integration business was hard. After looking at Mrs. Brown's scrapbook, I didn't know if I was brave enough to be friends with Ruby. She said I wasn't standing up for what was right, but I didn't want to quit eating at Bubba's or swimming in the town pool. And if we were gonna make up, I had to change. Our families had worked together as far back as anybody could remember. Calling Ruby that name was the meanest thing I could have said. I needed to think about the fine line, and what it meant to cross over it.

Chapter Eighteen

Ice-Cream Social

On Thursday afternoon, Granny and I broke and strung green beans underneath the maple trees.

"You've moped around here all day," she said. "Are you still worried about school?"

I snapped a fresh bean into three pieces. Mostly I was worried about Robin, but the thought of being the new kid at school was gnawing a hole in my stomach too. Would Ruby and I just ignore each other, nod our heads as if we barely knew one another? What did integration really mean here in Shady Creek?

Granny shifted her weight in the green webbed lawn

chair. "I guess it wouldn't help much if I told you things have a way of working themselves out."

"Nope, I would still be worried."

"Drucker will be there," Granny teased. "Won't that help some?"

My mouth fell open big enough to catch flies. How did Granny know I had a crush on Drucker?

Granny chuckled and peered into the garden bucket. "I notice everything about you, Sarah Beth Willis. You and Robin have my heart."

We were still stringing beans when Miss Irene hollered, "Miss Maybelle, you at home?"

"Under the maple trees," Granny answered. She sent me to fetch a chair for Miss Irene from the porch.

Miss Irene sat down and smoothed her faded dress over her knees. She kept working her mouth like she had something to say but couldn't quite get it out. "Miss Maybelle, I hate being beholden to anybody, even you, but I need a favor."

Granny snapped a bean and then looked up. "I'll surely help you if I can."

"I'm worried some of the mothers will act real ugly at the Back-to-School Ice-Cream Social. They're riled up over having a colored teacher. I heard about it over at Gentry's Grocery."

"I'm not surprised," Granny said, "not one bit, but how can we stop such as that?"

Miss Irene reached into her apron pocket. "I have a list of the children that will be in Mrs. Smyre's class right here. How about calling their parents? Remind 'em they're generally good people. Ask 'em to do what's right."

Granny reached for the list. "I don't think there's time for me to call all these people before tonight, but I'll call as many as I can. I'll start with the families I know are liable to be the biggest problem."

"That would surely ease my mind," Miss Irene said. "Pauline Smyre is a fine teacher. All she needs is a chance to get off on the right foot."

I remembered seeing Mrs. Smyre and her daughter the

day before. "Call Mrs. Brown at the library," I said. "She's on the committee. I bet she'd help call the parents."

"Sarah Beth, that's using your thinking cap," Granny said. "I'll start by talking to Mrs. Brown."

My new school was made of red brick and shaped like a long, skinny rectangle. The building sat in the middle of a big green lawn, with two baseball fields, seesaws, monkey bars, and swing sets. From the outside, it looked a lot nicer than the colored school. I remembered what Ruby said about wanting to go to a school with real playground equipment.

Grandpa turned the ignition off and put the keys in his pocket. "I'm going on to the cafeteria for refreshments," he said. "Y'all come on down after you meet Sarah's teacher."

I followed Granny inside. First through fifth grades were at one end of a long hall. We passed by an auditorium with a stage, red velvet curtains, and shiny wood floors. I hoped Ruby had seen it. I could picture her singing on that stage.

My new classroom was just past the auditorium, on the sixth-through-eighth-grade end of the hall. Granny pushed her spectacles up on her nose. "Mrs. Smyre," she read from the sign beside the door.

I squared my shoulders and marched inside. The room was jammed with parents and kids. I waited in line to meet Mrs. Smyre.

Her skin was the color of hot chocolate, same as Ruby's. Miss Irene stood beside her, wearing a royal-blue suit. Mrs. Smyre shook my hand. "I'm Mrs. Smyre, and you are . . . ?"

"Sarah. Sarah Beth Willis." I didn't tell her that I'd been spying on her the day before.

"Sarah Beth is almost like one of my grandbabies," Miss Irene said.

I felt good all over when she said that. If Ruby had told her about the terrible thing I said, Miss Irene had surely forgiven me, and if she had, maybe Ruby could too.

Mrs. Smyre gave me a warm smile. "Welcome to Shady Creek School. I am new here, just as you are."

I loved the new teacher's voice. It had rhythm, a storyteller's voice. "Ma'am, do you read aloud to your class?"

"On occasion. Why do you ask?"

I felt my face flush. "Ummm. Well, you have a good voice for it."

"Thank you, Sarah. That's the nicest compliment I've been paid today."

I moved to the back of the room and watched Mrs. Smyre greet each parent that walked in. She was bound to know some of them had threatened to cause a scene, but it didn't show in her face or her words.

When Ruby Lee walked in, I wanted to drink in the sight of her, but instead I turned to stare out the window. My stomach churned because of the mean name I'd called her.

I picked up a copy of the school calendar, while Granny chatted with Miss Irene and then with the other parents.

Betsy Carter's mama whispered to Granny, "I'm still not sure about a colored teacher."

I pretended to study the calendar, but I was all ears.

"We need to give Mrs. Smyre a fair shake," Granny said. "Times are changing, and we all have some adjusting to do." She took Mrs. Carter by the arm. "I'm on the welcoming committee. Let's me and you have us a chat with the new teacher."

After Mrs. Smyre shook hands with every parent, she stepped to the front of the room. She waited until all the chatter died down. "I've asked Mrs. Brown, Miss Irene, and Miss Maybelle to escort the grown-ups to the cafeteria so I can get to know the children. They'll join you for ice cream in about ten minutes."

There was lots of whispering, but with Granny, Mrs. Brown, and Miss Irene herding the parents like cattle, nobody had the guts to complain out loud. I was real curious to hear what the new teacher had to say.

I took a seat at one of the desks. "Welcome to seventh grade," Mrs. Smyre said.

Nobody answered her.

Silently, I counted three colored children: Ruby, a tall girl with cornrows, and a muscular boy with close-cropped hair. There were twenty-five white kids, including me.

"If you'll approach this year with open minds," Mrs. Smyre said, "we'll journey far past the banks of Shady Creek and take a trip around the globe." She pulled a map of the world down from its roller case. She pointed to a bookcase brimming with books, and then put her hand on a record player. "We'll learn about life in other countries, I'll introduce you to the works of great authors, and we'll listen to Duke Ellington and Ella Fitzgerald. I have great things in store for this class."

I kept my head down, but cut my eyes around the room. Not a single soul was watching Mrs. Smyre.

"Ah, boys and girls," she said. "Your avoiding me will never do." She turned an empty desk to face us and sat down. "I believe some of you are uneasy about school integration, and me in particular," she said.

I raised my head, and lots of other kids did too. We were curious to see what this unusual teacher would say and do next.

"Black and white folks are a little different on the outside," she continued. "But on the inside, we're just the same. We all need friends." And then she did something that caused our mouths to drop open. She invited each of us to touch her face and hair.

Betsy Carter squirmed, before sitting on her hands. Not one person volunteered to be first, but then I stood up. I wasn't a bit afraid to touch Mrs. Smyre, because I'd been touching Miss Irene and Ruby my whole life. I walked over and touched Mrs. Smyre's cheek. Her skin was soft, like satin. Then I patted her short, dark hair.

After I took my seat, curiosity got the best of the other kids. Everybody but the colored children lined up. I thought they were being plumb rude until Ruby explained. "We don't need to touch your hair," she said. "It's just like ours."

"I understand," Mrs. Smyre said, but then Ruby's friend raised her hand.

"Yes, Ella?"

Ella pointed her finger straight at me. "I'd rather touch her hair. Ruby says it feels like corn silk."

Ruby would know. When we were little, maybe six or seven, Ruby had asked to touch my freckles, and then she'd asked to touch my hair. When it'd been my turn to touch her, I had told Ruby she was the color of a candy bar. Since we both loved candy, we decided that was a good color to be.

Mrs. Smyre nodded at Ella. "Sarah Beth, would you mind if Ella touched your hair?"

I twisted a strand around my finger while I thought about it. "I reckon that would be okay."

Ella rose and touched my hair real gentle, like she was rubbing a baby chick. "Ruby was right," she said. "Just like corn silk."

I pushed through the crowded hall on my way to the cafeteria. Reverend Reece and Reverend Tyree from Miss Irene's church were patrolling the ice-cream social.

That seemed like a stroke of genius. I didn't think most folks would act out in front of their minister.

In the cafeteria, there were three lines for homemade ice cream. One for chocolate, one for vanilla, and one for strawberry. I waved to Granny standing in the vanilla line and went to check things out for myself. I searched the crowd for the only three people I knew: Betsy, Ruby Lee, and Drucker.

I saw Betsy first, standing with a group of "perfect girls." Perfect hair, perfect clothes, even a dab of makeup. As much as I liked Betsy, all that perfection made me feel bad about my freckles and ratty ponytail. I wished I'd worn my hair down and put on some Pink Passion lip gloss.

Next, I spotted Ruby Lee and Ella. They were standing with their own people. I counted sixteen girls and boys of different ages. All of them were dressed in their Sunday best. They weren't saying much, just looking down and shuffling their feet.

And finally, I saw Drucker. His hair was damp, like he'd just taken a shower. He was wearing a striped shirt tucked into a pair of Levi's. The boys standing around him had broad shoulders, probably football players. None of them were as cute as Drucker.

A yearning for home washed over me. I didn't have a group anymore, not like at my old school. I took the easy way out and walked over to Betsy. "Hey, Betsy."

"Hey, corn silk."

I didn't know how to take that until Betsy said, "Thanks for what you did in there. It was awful uncomfortable until you touched her first." Betsy gestured toward the two girls standing closest to her. "Lisa, Susan, this is Sarah Willis. She's new to Shady Creek."

"We're talking about cheerleading tryouts," Lisa said. "We're sick of all that integration business."

"Yeah," Susan piped in. "Betsy can do a cartwheel, a roundoff, a front split, and a side split. She's been practicing all summer."

Ruby and me kept watching each other, though we pretended not to. Miss Irene must have taken the hot comb to her hair. When we were little, she'd run and hide to avoid it. I listened for a few minutes as Betsy, Susan, and Lisa talked about cheerleading. I didn't have much interest in it; the school newspaper was more my speed. I wondered how long three girls could talk about pom-poms. The answer seemed to be forever. Betsy and her friends didn't even notice when I mumbled an excuse and slipped away.

Maybe I couldn't be school friends with Ruby, but it seemed downright mean to ignore her. I mustered up my courage and fought my way through the crowded cafeteria. "Hi, Ruby."

All the chatter died down in her group. Ruby's dark eyes met my green ones. I knew exactly what she was thinking: *I told you we couldn't be school friends.*

After what seemed like forever, Ruby said, "Hey there." She didn't bother introducing me to the boys and girls from the colored school. Ella gave me a nice smile, before looking away.

I felt whiter than white. Like I was somehow responsible for the town pool and Bubba's Grill, and every other bad thing a white person had ever done to a black one.

Finally, Ruby spoke up. "How's Robin doing?"

"She's back in the hospital. They took her cast off, and she's working with a physical therapist. Thank you for helping us this summer."

"You're welcome," Ruby said. "The money will come in handy." She turned toward Ella. "I did some cleaning and gardening for the Willis family this summer."

So that's how it is, I thought. *Ruby and me are gonna be just like Granny and Miss Irene. We're gonna smile and nod when we see each other in public. Anything else is too hard.* "I'm glad the money helped." My bottom lip started to tremble, and I bit down on it.

"I got your letter," Ruby said. "I appreciate what you wrote, but it didn't change my mind about things."

Tears welled up in my eyes so that Ruby and her friends became a blur. I turned my back on them. I bobbed and weaved my way through the crowd to a poster on the cafeteria wall. It was of a night sky, a full moon, and some dried cornstalks. If I stared at it long enough, maybe I wouldn't cry.

What: The Harvest Moon School Dance

Who: 6th, 7th, and 8th Graders

When: Friday, October 3, from 7–10 p.m.

"Are you going?"

"What?" I whirled around and bumped into Drucker.

"Ouch!" He rubbed his forehead. "To the dance. Are you going?"

"Uh, well, uh, I don't know."

Drucker kept rubbing his forehead. "You're new. How are you gonna make friends if you don't go to the dance?"

I shrugged. All I could think about was the name I had called Ruby Lee, the stuff in Mrs. Brown's scrapbook, and how Ruby thought I was more like a chicken than a Freedom Rider.

Drucker put his hands in his pockets and rocked back on his heels. "You can't make friends staring at a poster."

Tears were pricking my eyes, because I didn't fit in with Betsy's group or with Ruby's. No way I wanted to cry in front of him. "I ha-have to go."

"Hey, wait up," Drucker called.

I hurried across the gym to find Grandpa. I didn't even look back.

A big crowd had gathered in the parking lot. "Wonder what's going on?" I asked.

Granny shook her head. "It can't be anything good."

The dead silence was what bothered me the most. Normally, anywhere there's a lot of people, there's a lot of noise.

"Sarah, stay behind me," Grandpa said, but when I saw Ruby pushing her way through the sea of people, I followed her.

The first thing I noticed was that Mrs. Smyre had a run in her stockings. Her dress was wrinkled too, and she'd lost an earring.

"No, no, I wasn't hurt," she assured Reverend Tyree. "Just saw a group of hoodlums gathered around my car. I chased them off, but shouldn't have been running in the dark with high heels." She reached up and pulled a leaf out of her hair.

I noticed that most people weren't looking at Mrs. Smyre but staring at her car. Somebody had keyed the awful word across the side. The same one I'd called Ruby Lee. The tears I'd been fighting back all night finally came. There was no way to stop them. I was crying for

Ruby, for me, for Mrs. Smyre, and for all the people in my town, even the bad ones who'd vandalized the car.

Ruby was standing underneath the floodlights so I could see her real good. Her shoulders were hunched over her chest. She rocked from side to side, while the tears streaked down her face.

Some nights make you question if there really is a God in heaven. I hung my head, feeling more hopeless than I ever had before, but then Mrs. Smyre's voice rang out. She sang the words to "We Shall Overcome." Reverend Tyree took one of her hands and Reverend Reece took the other one. Then lots of people started singing. White or black, it made no difference, everybody's voices blended. The notes to that song soared past the treetops until they reached the starry sky. I remembered a quote from one of Dr. King's speeches: *Darkness cannot drive out darkness; only light can do that.* It might be a bumpy ride, but our school was headed toward integration.

CHAPTER NINETEEN

A Brave Girl

Sunday morning was quiet as a whisper until Rowdy started barking.

"I was hoping for a peaceful morning," Granny said. She pulled the gingham curtains back and peeked out the kitchen window. "It's Hiram Fletcher."

I rolled the biscuit dough between my palms while Granny waited for him by the back door. "Morning, Hiram. Can I get you a cup of coffee?"

"No, no time for coffee. My cows are loose. I was wondering if George could help Drucker and me round them up."

Drucker. I hadn't seen him since the ice-cream social, or Ruby either. I was still trying to make sense of all that had happened that night.

Granny said to Mr. Fletcher, "Sure, George would be glad to help you. That's what neighbors are for. He's out at the barn doing up the morning chores."

A few minutes later, Grandpa hurried into the kitchen, carrying a full pail of milk. "Don't hold breakfast for me," he said. "Hiram's waiting for me in his truck. No telling where those fool cows have taken off to."

Granny walked with Grandpa to the door. "Sarah and I are gonna drive your truck and go on to church," she said. "Good luck with the cows."

I kept working the dough and worrying over Ruby Lee. School would be starting tomorrow. Maybe I needed to get my courage up and go see her.

Granny came back into the kitchen and strained the milk. "You had a restless night. I got up to check on you a couple of times."

"I didn't sleep well. I kept waking up, thinking about all the bad things that have happened."

Granny poured herself a cup of coffee and sat down at the table. "No need to fry the ham until you get the biscuits in the oven. Want to talk about the stuff that's worrying you?"

"No."

Granny sighed, and I worked the dough. I pinched some off and rolled it into a circle. I placed the biscuit into a shiny greased pan, and then made eleven more.

"I'll get the oven door," Granny said. "Careful now, don't get burned." She pulled the door open, bumping her leg hard against the corner. Her crepe-like skin tore. Blood ran from her knotty veins.

I dropped the pan of biscuits and sat down hard on the floor. I covered my eyes, but all I could see was blood. I heard squealing tires and smelled burning rubber.

"Sarah, Sarah Beth." Granny's voice came to me as if through a fog. "Help me, child. Ain't nobody else here."

"I-I can't."

"Yes, you can. Grab a clean dishtowel and press it against my leg."

I shook my head, trying to fight off the bad memories.

Granny kept calling my name. "Sarah, Sarah Beth, help me child."

I wrung my hands, but finally did as Granny asked, pressing a checked dishtowel against her leg. The blood quickly soaked through it. I grabbed another towel, and blood soaked through it too.

"Need a doctor," Granny moaned.

The blood pooled on the floor. *Think! Think!*

Thickening, I could use thickening! Granny used flour to make corn and potatoes creamier. And flour soaked up the buttermilk when I made biscuits.

I grabbed the flour bin and started heaping clean white flour on Granny's leg. It formed a red, gooey mess. I put a towel on top and pressed down. I kept heaping flour and applying more pressure.

"It's working," Granny said. "It's working."

The kitchen floor had turned into a sloppy mess of blood and flour. "Granny, I'm gonna call an ambulance."

"It'll take too long. Everybody gets lost out here."

"Okay, I'll try and find Grandpa."

"He could be anywhere in these hills and hollers." Granny put her hand on my cheek. "You're gonna have to drive me to the hospital."

"I'm scared."

"Me too, but I'm counting on you. Hurry!"

I raced across the farmyard and climbed into the truck. My hand reached for the ignition, but the keys were missing. *Think! Think!* Maybe they were in Grandpa's bedroom.

I rushed back to the house with tears streaming down my cheeks.

"What's wrong?" Granny asked.

"I can't find the keys!" I sprinted down the hall. The keys weren't on Grandpa's night table. They weren't on his dresser either. *Think! Think!*

I ran to the den. The keys weren't on top of the television or on the corner shelf. *Think! Think!*

I tore through the bathroom, knocking over a bottle of Old Spice shaving lotion. I kept running!

My sides ached. I bent over to catch my breath. *Think! Think!* The floor mat. I should have looked under the floor mat in Grandpa's truck.

I bolted out the front door, across the porch, and through the farmyard. I jerked open the door and pulled back the gray floor mat. There was nothing underneath it but dirt.

I pounded the steering wheel, screaming in frustration. I looked up toward heaven to beg for some help. And then I saw them! Grandpa's keys were dangling from the visor!

I snatched them down and started the truck. Slamming it into gear, I roared across the yard, skidding to a stop by the back door. I left the truck idling, rushed inside, and helped Granny to her feet. She leaned against my shoulder as we hobbled out the door. The towels came loose and the bleeding started again. I practically hoisted her into the truck.

"Didn't know you were so strong," she mumbled.

I raced back inside for flour and more towels. Packing Granny's leg again, I pressed until the bleeding was under control. Then I jumped into the driver's seat and took off.

My palms were sweating. I drove with my left hand and wiped my right hand on my shorts. Then I changed hands. My shoulders ached, and I lifted them up and lowered them down. The blasted truck would only go thirty-five miles per hour! I wiped my palms again. Every time I hit a bump in the road Granny groaned.

I alternated between watching the road and sneaking quick glances at Granny. Her head rolled back against the seat. One thing was lucky: Because it was so early on a Sunday morning, there was hardly any traffic on the road. I kept driving and started praying. It was only two words over and over. "Help me, help me, help me, help me!"

Finally, we left the fields behind, headed toward Tucker. Traffic picked up a little, and I had to concentrate on my driving. With a red light just ahead, I laid on the horn and eased off the gas pedal. There were no cars coming from either direction, so I floored it, and ran the light. "Help me, help me, help me."

A wailing siren set my teeth on edge. In the rearview mirror, I saw a police car barreling down on us.

I pressed on the horn and didn't stop.

The scowling policeman pulled up beside me.

I drove with my left hand and pointed at Granny with my right. I yelled through the open window. "Hospital. Bad accident."

The policeman motioned for me to follow as he passed the truck. He led me through town with his siren blaring. The few drivers on the road pulled off on the right side. I kept my eyes glued to the police car, following it all the way to the emergency room entrance.

I continued blowing the horn, and doctors ran through the hospital's sliding glass doors. The policeman helped them load Granny on a stretcher.

Granny opened her eyes. "Sarah, you're a brave girl," she whispered.

I sat on an orange plastic chair in the waiting room. A blond, curly-haired nurse left her seat from behind the desk and brought me a box of Kleenex.

"Is there anything I can do to help?" she asked.

I wiped my eyes and mumbled, "Could you check on my granny? She cut her leg and they brought her in on a stretcher."

The nurse patted me on the shoulder. "I'll see what I can do. In the meantime, try to relax. I'll be back shortly."

I sat on the hard chair for what seemed like forever and a day. Finally, the nurse walked over and bent down in front of me again. "They're stitching up your granny's leg. They want to give her a pint of blood and keep her here overnight, but she's going to be just fine."

The policeman strode back into the waiting room. For the first time, I really looked at him. He had a crew cut, and his uniform was starched and pressed to perfection. I had a funny urge to salute him.

The patrolman pulled up a chair in front of me and took a pen and pad from his pocket. "It's about time we were properly introduced," he said. "You can call me Sergeant Scott."

"And you can call me Sarah."

"Well, Sarah, do you have your license handy?"

I looked down at the floor and squirmed in my chair. "Sergeant Scott, I'm only twelve. I don't have a license."

"That's what I was afraid of," he said. "I need for you to give me a statement about what happened."

I started with making biscuits and went through the whole morning.

"Whew!" Sergeant Scott said. "That's what I call having a bad day." Then he winked at me. "I grew up on a farm myself. It's a good thing you know how to drive."

I flopped back in my chair and smiled. "Uh, sir, am I in trouble for driving without a license?"

He smiled back at me, and his blue eyes twinkled. "Not this time. I'm calling it 'extenuating circumstances' in my report. Do I have your solemn promise that you won't drive in town again until you get your license?"

"Yes, sir!"

"Well now, Sarah, I can either give you a ride home or call your parents."

"I don't need a ride home. My parents are right here in the hospital. My sister is Robin Willis, the little girl who was hit by the car."

"I read about that in the newspaper," Sergeant Scott said. "I'll talk to the receptionist and have your dad paged." Sergeant Scott shook my hand. "Good-bye, Sarah. You're a brave girl."

A brave girl. A brave girl. This time, I was a brave girl.

The receptionist paged my dad: "Mr. Charles Willis. Please come to the emergency room. Mr. Charles Willis."

I stared out the window while I waited on Dad. There was a big commotion when he stormed the front desk.

"I'm Charles Willis," he yelled. "What's wrong? What's going on?"

Uh-oh. Dad looked like somebody had stepped on his last nerve. I hurried across the waiting room. "Dad, calm down. I can explain everything."

He threw his arms around me and hugged me so tight I was afraid he'd break a couple of my ribs. "Uh, Dad, I can't breathe."

He just kept hugging. "Sarah Beth, I'm about to have a heart attack. Why in the devil did you have me paged to the emergency room?"

I led Dad over to the row of orange chairs so we could sit down. "It's a long story."

"I've got time," he said.

I told him about Granny cutting her leg on the oven door.

"She shoulda had that leg looked at a long time ago," he said.

Then I told him about the flour.

"Flour? What made you think of using flour?"

A doctor in a white coat with a stethoscope around his neck walked up beside Dad. "I'm interested in the answer to that question too," he said. The doctor stuck his hand out. "I'm Doctor Wood, and you must be the family of Maybelle Willis."

Dad stood up and shook the doctor's hand. "I'm Charlie Willis, Maybelle's son. And this is her granddaughter, Sarah."

The doctor looked like Clark Kent. I imagined him changing clothes in a telephone booth.

"Maybelle is doing just fine," he said. "We've cleaned the wound and stitched it up. I want to keep her overnight and have a specialist take a look at her leg. He can recommend treatment options to avoid another emergency situation. But what I really want to hear about is the flour. In all my years of medicine, I've never seen anything like it."

I didn't think it was so unusual, just good common sense. "Granny has been teaching me to cook this summer. When I make biscuits, I add flour and buttermilk to form dough. The more flour I add, the drier the dough becomes. I figured the blood was like buttermilk, and if I added enough flour, it would form a good, stiff dough and soak up the blood."

"Ingenious," Dr. Wood said. "Young lady, if not for your quick thinking, the situation with your grandmother could have been very serious."

Dad slung his arm around my shoulders. "I'm proud of you, and your mama will be proud too."

I grinned. "You don't know the half of it. Grandpa wasn't home, and I drove Granny here in his truck."

"Lord have mercy!" Dad said. "I'd better find your grandpa." He squeezed my shoulders. "Sarah Beth, what am I gonna do with you? You're growing up way too fast."

Chapter Twenty

Sarah Comes Clean

We were packed like sardines in Robin's tiny hospital room. Mama and Grandpa sat in chairs on either side of her bed, while Dad and I leaned against the wall beside the door.

"Maybe I should train Sarah to be a race car driver," Grandpa said. "With her drivin' and my expert instruction, she could give ol' Richard Petty a run for his money."

"If you're gonna train Sarah to be a race car driver," Dad joked, "you'd better buy a faster truck."

Dad and Grandpa were being silly. Guess we all needed some relief from accidents and hospitals.

"I better go check on Maybelle," Grandpa said. "I have a notion that woman is being a terrible patient. Soon as they turn their backs, she'll be runnin' the hospital kitchen."

"Sarah, you're a hero," Robin said, "like Marshal Dillon."

I looked down at my sneakers. A hero would tell the truth, but the longer I waited, the harder it was to come clean.

"I'm thirsty," Robin said.

I noticed the cot pushed against the window. "Is this where you sleep?" I asked Mama.

Mama poured some water for Robin and put a straw into the glass. "Yes, we've never left her alone. The hospital has been very good about that."

I stretched and yawned. "Could I take a nap?"

Mama nodded her okay, and pretty soon I was fast asleep.

I dreamed of Robin in a leg brace and built-up shoes. Mean kids were pointing and laughing. When I jerked awake, her bed was empty. I threw the covers off and sat up. "Where is Robin?"

"Sssh," Mama said. "Calm down. She's gone to physical therapy."

All the breath left my body in a big whoosh. "How's Granny?"

Mama got up from her chair and hugged me. "Relax. Granny's fine." She patted my back. "I'm very proud of you. I hope you know that."

"Yeah, I know." I blinked back tears. Even saving Granny wasn't enough to make up for Robin's accident. Nothing was.

Mama reached into her pocket for a comb and dragged it through my tangled hair. "You have a guest in the waiting room," she said.

"Me? Who would come to see me here?"

"Ruby Lee," Mama answered.

I stood in the waiting room doorway, staring at Ruby. I wasn't sure what she wanted or why she was here. I was afraid to hope for something good.

Ruby stared back.

I outlasted her in the staring contest, and Ruby finally trudged over. "You need to listen up, because I'm not much good at apologizing. I'm sorry about everything. About telling your secret, about the mean things I said, and how I acted at the ice-cream social. I've been ashamed of myself all summer."

"Me too. I shouldn't have called you that awful word. When I saw it scratched on Mrs. Smyre's car, it hurt so much I could barely breathe."

"I know. That's how it was for me too." Ruby looked into my eyes. "When it's just you and me, it's easy to be friends. But at school, I'm not sure how to go about it. We're like two mismatched socks."

I gave Ruby's hand a quick squeeze. Two men about Grandpa's age saw me touch her and frowned. I figured the best thing to do was ignore them. Ruby was right about two socks, one brown and one white. I wasn't sure how to handle school either, but I wanted to try. "Maybe Mrs. Smyre could help us with being friends at school. Mrs. Brown in the library gave me the idea."

"I hadn't thought of that," Ruby said. "Maybe she could." Ruby smiled, and I could tell we were back to normal, or at least as close to normal as we could be, with school integration looming. "How's Miss Maybelle doing?" she asked.

"Pretty good. They stitched her up and gave her a pint of blood. How'd you find out about Granny's accident, anyway?"

"My uncle Clarence saw you drive through town. He followed and watched them bring Miss Maybelle in on a stretcher. My granny's visiting with yours right now. We came to help."

I thought about the blood and flour all over the kitchen floor. Miss Irene would make short work of that.

Ruby and I walked over and sat by the windows. We

were quiet for a few minutes, but then Ruby turned her mischievous smile on me. "Enough of this serious talk. I've got a newsflash for you."

"What's that?"

"You know the other night when Drucker tried to talk to you?"

"Yeah."

"He was fixing to ask you to the Harvest Moon."

"The school dance? No way!"

Ruby nodded. "He sure enough was."

I squinted and eyed Ruby suspiciously. "How do you know?"

"Because Curtis told me."

"Curtis is one of your friends from church, right?"

Ruby laughed. "Curtis is my boyfriend, only he doesn't know it yet! I've been telling him what to do his whole life. I already told him he's taking me to the Harvest Moon."

I felt my eyes bug out. "You did? What'd he say?"

"He called me Miss Bossy Britches. But then I put the

evil eye on him, and he said, 'Somebody has to take you so it might as well be me.' "

I shook my head. Leave it to Ruby to make her own luck. "Okay, 'Miss Bossy Britches,' how does Curtis know Drucker was gonna ask me?"

"Well, it's like this: The boys on the football team have been practicing together for about a month now. It's taking a while, but they're finally becoming friends. Drucker told Curtis at practice how he was gonna ask you, but when you ran off, ol' Drucker lost his nerve."

"Ah, Ruby! I want to go with Drucker, and now I've really messed up."

"Don't you worry," she said. "I can fix it. I'll have a talk with Curtis and tell him you'll say yes. Then Curtis will talk to Drucker, and before you know it, you'll have a date for the dance."

I loved the excitement in Ruby's eyes. I hoped none of the grown-ups would get all worked up about integration and ruin our first school dance.

When I opened the door to Robin's hospital room, Mama looked up from her sewing. "Did you have a nice visit with Ruby Lee?"

"Yeah, it was good." I didn't tell Mama how Ruby and me were gonna be school friends. I didn't want to hear about the fine line. Just for today, I wanted to be happy that Ruby was my best friend again.

Mama put her sewing down and stretched her arms over her head. "My fingers could use a break. Let's take a peek at Robin's physical therapy."

We walked past the nurses' station to a group of elevators. I hated the way the hospital smelled. It reminded me of the alcohol nurses used to swab my arm, just before a shot.

Mama nodded and smiled to several people on the elevator and on the physical therapy floor. We passed by people in wheelchairs and others pushing IV poles. Mama stopped before a door midway down the hall. A sign beside it said P.T. Mama opened the door just wide enough for me to look inside.

Robin held on to two parallel bars. A woman in a white uniform stood ready to catch her if she fell. Robin hopped on her left leg, with her right leg bent at the knee.

"The doctors are trying to get her strong enough to use crutches," Mama said.

Robin didn't look up. She used all her concentration on the bars.

Mama strained forward, as if she were trying to help Robin move along. "Physical therapy is hard work," she said. "Robin is exhausted when her session's over."

Every muscle in Robin's body looked rigid. Her teeth were clenched.

"She's the one who is brave," I said.

Mama peeked over my shoulder. "Robin is scared and brave at the same time. She's scared because she can't walk yet, but she's brave enough to work hard so someday she'll be able to."

I finally understood. Courage is doing hard things when you're most afraid, like saying you're sorry, or being friends with a colored girl. I kept watching Robin struggle, and thought how lucky I was to still have a little sister. All that love filled my chest, rising like a perfect pan of biscuits.

Robin looked up and saw us peeking in the door. She stuck her tongue out and made a funny face.

I laughed and made one right back. I thought of what Ruby had said. "*I'm not much good at apologizing.*" I wasn't much good at it either, but I owed my sister a big one.

In Robin's hospital room, *Gunsmoke* played on the television suspended from the ceiling.

"Sarah, stop pacing," Mama said.

I forced myself to sit down. I curled and uncurled my fists.

Robin watched the show as if she'd been hypnotized.

When it came to an end, she looked sad. "What if I walk with a limp?" she asked. "Can I still be a cowgirl?"

Mama continued hemming a pair of pants. "In the very old episodes of *Gunsmoke*, there's a character called Chester, and he walked with a limp."

"That's good to know," Robin said. "Maybe I'll walk like Chester."

Mama finished hemming one leg and started on the other. "That's right. You can still be a cowgirl whether you have a limp or not."

I didn't want Robin to have a limp. I just wanted my sister back exactly the way she used to be, but that was impossible. It was like Ruby said: *"Some stuff can't be fixed."*

Dad stuck his head in the door of Robin's room. "I'm going to the cafeteria for a cup of coffee." He looked over at Mama. "Can I bring you back one?"

"No!" I said. "Please don't go for coffee. I have something important to tell you, and it can't wait."

Mama stopped sewing and folded the pants in her lap.

Dad frowned, and his eyebrows drew close together. He walked in and closed the door. "What's wrong?" he asked.

"Just let me think for a minute." I started pacing again, then stopped and closed my eyes. I decided the best way was to get it over with. To jump right in like at the town pool when the water was too cold. I mustered up all my courage. "Robin's accident was my fault," I blurted out.

Mama shook her head. "No, don't be silly. Absolutely not."

I crossed my arms over my chest. "This is so hard. Please, please don't interrupt. Just let me finish."

Mama and Dad stared at each other. Both of them nodded for me to go ahead.

"On the day of the accident, I was reading a library book. When I looked up, Robin was gone. If I had paid more attention, maybe this wouldn't have happened."

Mama's eyes were brimming with tears.

Dad stared at the floor.

Robin's mouth flew open in surprise.

Nobody said a single word.

I spun around and jerked open the door.

"Wait!" Robin called.

I ignored her and rushed down the hall.

"Sarah, stop!" Dad yelled.

His footsteps thundered behind me. I raced by the nurses' station.

The woman at the desk called, "No running in the halls, please."

I passed by doctors and patients roaming the hall. Tears blinded me as I turned a corner to the right.

Dad's footsteps sounded closer.

I picked up speed, but he was gaining on me.

Closer, closer, closer.

My shirt stretched taut as he grabbed it from behind.

Dad turned me around to face him. "Sweet pea, you can't run away from your problems. You've got to face 'em head-on."

"I'm so sorry. I didn't mean for Robin to get hurt."

Dad pulled me into his arms. "Sssh," he said. He patted my back just like I was a baby. I cried against his chest until his shirt was sopping wet. Sorrow was overwhelming me, like in Ruby's song.

When my sobs turned to sniffles, Dad wiped my face with his handkerchief. "Come with me. It's high time we settled this."

I trudged beside Dad back to Robin's room. I hoped my parents would still love me as much as before, and Granny and Grandpa too. I hoped Robin could forgive me.

Dad opened the door and gave me a gentle push into the room.

Mama looked up, with tears shining on her cheeks. "Sarah, it was an accident. We've never blamed you."

"B-b-b-but, I blame myself."

Robin scooted over to make room for me. "Sit here," she said.

I sat on the edge of the bed and took Robin's hand. I looked down, too ashamed to meet her eyes. "I'm—I'm so sorry. I've been trying to make it up to you all summer, but I can't find a way."

Robin's chubby hand reached out and wiped the tears off my face. "I ran away on purpose."

"What?"

Dad moved closer to Robin. "Why?" he asked. "Why would you do such a thing?"

Robin squirmed and pulled on one of her curls. "Cause of Scruffy. He was outside at Cathy's, and I wanted to play with him." She quit messing with her hair and shook her finger at me. "Sarah always tells me NO. She says, 'Wait until Mama gets home.' I ran away when she wasn't looking."

Robin had raced full speed ahead without checking for danger, but that was no excuse. I shouldn't have been reading. I had known better than that.

"We make rules to keep you safe," Dad said. "I need you to promise that you won't ever run away again." He didn't quit staring until Robin promised.

Mama stood up and put her hand on my shoulder.

"Sarah, the police report says the driver was going too fast for a residential neighborhood. If you insist on placing blame, there's plenty of it to go around."

Inside my head, the screaming siren played over and over like a scratched record. Maybe someday my flashbacks would fade. I hoped so.

"That young man made a terrible mistake," Mama said, "but it won't do any good to look back." She reached for a Kleenex from Robin's bedside table and wiped her eyes. "There are a lot of what-ifs here. If only I hadn't been working in the garden. If only Sarah hadn't been reading. If only Cathy hadn't let Scruffy out of the house. Let's put all the what-ifs behind us."

I wanted to. I wanted to feel as shiny inside as a new penny.

Mama moved between Robin and me. She took each of us by the hand. Dad grabbed my other hand and Robin's too.

"Sarah, look at me," Mama said. "The accident is in the past. What's important now?"

I needed to get this right. I remembered the rest of Ruby's song.

Sorrow's overwhelmin' me
Lord, show me how to set it free.

I needed a gift from my family. I squeezed Mama and Dad's hands, but looked straight into Robin's eyes. "Forgiveness," I whispered. "Forgiveness is what matters now."

Chapter Twenty-One

Goodnight Moon

All alone with Scruffy, I sat on the steps, looking up at the full moon. I listened to the crickets chirping and the owls hooting. I didn't think there was a more peaceful place on earth.

The screen door creaked open. "Don't stay up too late," Dad said. "We have to bring Robin home from the hospital tomorrow."

Scruffy and I gazed at the stars. "Star light, star bright, first star I see tonight." I remembered my wishes. First, that Robin would be good as new. And then my second wish, that the accident would somehow not be my fault. My wishes hadn't come true, at least not exactly.

The doctors said Robin would walk with crutches for a while. She would have to work hard at physical therapy. Mama had ordered a brace and special shoes. Even so, there were no guarantees.

I had wished with all my heart for the accident not to be my fault. But I had made a big mistake. I reached into my pocket and pulled out an assignment from Mrs. Smyre. I was supposed to write an essay on how I had spent my summer vacation. Most years this would have been easy enough. I would have written about swimming lessons, 4-H Camp, and our annual trip to the beach. But this was far from a typical summer. I felt older now, maybe even old. That's what I would write my essay about.

I thought about each member of my family and how they loved me in a forever way. I remembered the wild ride with Granny to the hospital and finally telling the truth to my parents. I thought about Ruby Lee and how we were gonna be brave at school. I had found courage, just like the lion in *The Wizard of Oz*.

Some stuff still remained a mystery though. Like why my heart beat faster when Drucker smiled, or how faith worked, or why school integration had to be so hard. I didn't think I'd ever understand those things, even if I lived to be as old as Granny.

Scruffy scooted closer to me and howled. "*Aaiiee! Aaiiee!*" It was that time of night again. He was missing Robin too.

"Don't cry, Scruff. We're gonna be all right. I even have a date." I closed my eyes and thought of a new bedtime story for Robin. I grabbed my leather-bound journal to write.

Author's Note

In 1967, I started first grade. That was also the first year that the school system in Yadkin County, North Carolina, became integrated. Mrs. Pauline Porter was Fall Creek Elementary School's first African American teacher. She taught first grade in the classroom beside mine.

Mrs. Porter had a special gift for working with reluctant readers. So every afternoon, she changed classrooms with my teacher and worked with those of us struggling to read. Mrs. Porter had a beautiful cadence to her voice, and it reminded me of poetry.

Several years ago, I heard that Mrs. Porter was in failing health. I went for a visit to let her know what an impact she had made on my life. During that visit, she reminded me that white children had been uneasy about having a black teacher. To ease our concerns, she had asked each of us to touch her face and hair. As Mrs. Porter spoke, my mind drifted back to that time. I remembered how soft her skin felt and how she loved all children regardless of color. As a writer, I wanted to tell a story I hoped would pay tribute to her gentle dignity.

When I sat down to write, Mrs. Porter's story converged with another event from my childhood. In the summer of 1969, my younger sister was struck by a car. I was eight years old, but my childhood effectively ended that day. I had always known that bad things happened in the world, but after Robin's accident, I knew they could happen to my family.

My primary memory of that time period is guilt. Unlike Sarah, I was not a middle schooler, nor was I babysitting, but I felt guilty that I could run, and jump, and play, while Robin was stuck in a body cast.

As I wove the story of Robin's accident together with school integration, I was struck by the themes they have in common: courage and forgiveness.

Though inspired by actual events, this book is a work of fiction. I've created characters and changed what really happened in the interest of good storytelling. Most especially, the vandalism I wrote about did not take place in my hometown.

I also altered one tiny piece of history. My grandmother adored the soap opera *All My Children*, and so I included it even though the first episode didn't actually run until 1970.

I've been asked if I'm Sarah Beth Willis. The truth is there's a little bit of me in all the characters I create, but, no, I'm not Sarah Beth. At her age, I was neither aware of events outside my hometown, nor nearly as brave as she is. I've given Sarah the knowledge and courage I wish I'd had and that I wish for all my readers.

Acknowledgments

First and foremost I owe a hug and a thousand kisses to my husband, David. Without his encouragement and financial support, I would have never written a publishable word. Once I had the time to write, two novelists, Cynthia Chapman Willis and Joyce Sweeney, taught me the ropes. I found a cheering squad with critique mates Diana Sharp, Joni Klein-Higger, Eileen Goldenberg, and Nancy Stewart. Carolyn Coman's sage advice sparked the revision that ultimately sold to Scholastic. She said, "Take out everything that doesn't have your heart." Good advice for writing and in life.

Society of Children's Book Writers and Illustrators Florida chapter provided the initial contact with my editor, Andrea Pinkney, at their Orlando Conference. Andrea pushed me to delve even deeper into topics that made me uncomfortable, topics that made me cry. My agent, Deborah Warren, sealed the deal.

The pictures in the back of *Ruby Lee & Me* would not have been possible without the help of my cousin Tracy Williams, who took the photo of my grandparents' house, and Curtis Sponsler, who enhanced pictures from my childhood and reformatted them for publication.

Now it's time for my book to make its way into the world. With a grateful heart, I thank each of you who helped *Ruby Lee & Me* along the journey.

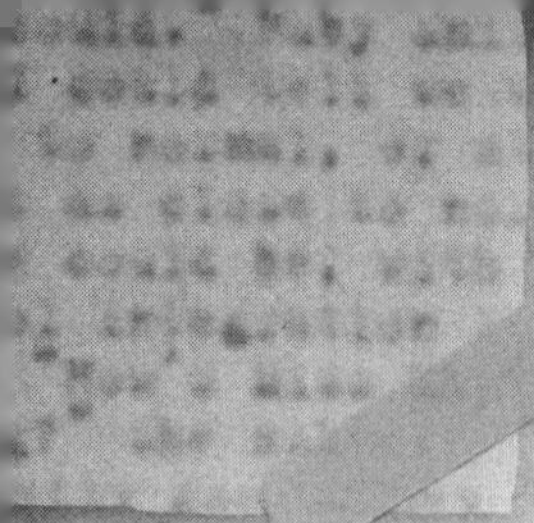

I had always loved my sister, but before the accident, I didn't know how much.

PAGE 33

Robin and me on my birthday.

There were no signs, and no streetlights. We passed the shadows of cow pastures, tobacco barns, and cornfields.

PAGE 9

An aerial view of my grandparents' farm.

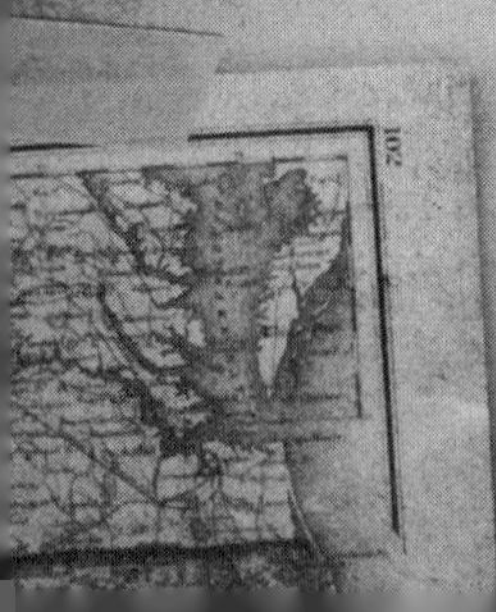

Though I didn't live there, the farm felt like a second home to me. Granny had left the front-porch light on for us, but only the moon shone on the barn and outbuildings.

PAGE 10

My grandparents' house.

My granny thought a hot meal would help almost any problem.

PAGE 11

Robin with our grandparents Rob and Cleo Williams.

I loved the new teacher's voice. It had rhythm, a storyteller's voice.

PAGE 160

Mrs. Pauline Porter was Fall Creek Elementary School's first African American teacher. She taught me to read.

"We need a project to keep our hands busy," Granny said. "If you'll get my sewing basket from the corner shelf, we'll make a surprise for Robin."

PAGE 146

My grandmother embroidered these horses on a pillowcase for Robin. We cut them off and framed them when the pillowcase had worn out.

"Having a pony would help her get well." I was sure of it.

PAGE 99

Robin riding Surelick. She eventually recovered from the accident and won lots of trophies riding him.

Shannon Hitchcock

is the author of the critically acclaimed *The Ballad of Jessie Pearl*, hailed for its immediacy and cadenced voice. This novel's story is based on Shannon's real-life experience and the teacher who inspired her as a child. Shannon's picture book biography, *Overgrown Jack*, was nominated for the Sue Alexander Most Promising New Work Award. Her writing has been published in *Cricket*, *Highlights for Children*, and *Children's Writer*. She lives in Tampa, Florida.

Friends of the
Houston Public Library

HITCH FLT
Hitchcock, Shannon.
Ruby lee and me.

01/16